Weekly Reader

Children's Book Club

EDUCATION CENTER • COLUMBUS 16, OHIO

Presents

The Rising Arrow

By HUGHIE CALL

ILLUSTRATED BY JACOB LANDAU

THE
Rising Arrow

BY HUGHIE CALL

ILLUSTRATED BY JACOB LANDAU

THE VIKING PRESS

NEW YORK · 1955

WEEKLY READER

Children's Book Club

Edition, 1955

PRINTED IN THE UNITED STATES OF AMERICA

AMERICAN BOOK–STRATFORD PRESS, INC., NEW YORK

For my grandsons

Gerry, Tommy, and Peter

Special Notice to Book Club Members

★ This book is a selection of the WEEKLY READER CHILDREN'S BOOK CLUB. It was chosen for you by the Editors and Selection Committee of *My Weekly Reader*, the most famous school newspaper in the world.

Members of the WEEKLY READER CHILDREN'S BOOK CLUB receive six or more exciting books during the year — including one or more Free Bonus Books upon joining. They also receive a Membership Certificate, Club Bookmarks and regular Book Club Bulletins.

We hope you enjoy this book and that you will tell your friends about the WEEKLY READER CHILDREN'S BOOK CLUB. They will want to become members, too!

WEEKLY READER
Children's Book Club
EDUCATION CENTER, COLUMBUS 16, OHIO

Contents

The Rising Arrow

A 1955 Selection of the

WEEKLY READER

Children's Book Club

EDUCATION CENTER, COLUMBUS 16, OHIO

1. Invitation
to a Montana Ranch

We heard from Uncle Emmet in May, just a month after the Defense Department had telegraphed that Dad was missing in Korea. Dan and I took the letter to Mother, and after she looked at the postmark—Virginia City, Montana—her face lighted up almost the way it used to, and she said, "Boys, it's from Uncle Emmet Whitney."

Dan and I hung around impatiently while she tore open the envelope. After she'd read the letter she sat there thinking a minute; then she said, "I've got to make a decision and you must help me. You're the men of the house until Dad returns."

She always tried to make us believe that Dad would come back, but sometimes there was a scared look in her eyes, and in the night we'd hear her pacing back and forth in her room. We knew she was afraid. And so were we, but we tried not to let her see.

"Read the letter aloud, Jack." She handed me a single sheet of lined tablet paper with big, scrawling writing all over it. I read:

"Dear Niece:

"I take my pen in hand to say I was sorry to hear the bad news you got from the Defense Department. Now, Helen, don't let it get you down. I got a feeling that Paul will make out and you'll be hearing from him one of these fine days. But the waiting won't be easy, and I got a suggestion to make. Why don't you and the two boys pack up and come spend the summer with me? My ranch is up in the mountains, but I've got a telephone. When word comes from Paul your Missouri operator can have it sent through to my phone. You call me collect and tell me when to expect you, and so there'll be no delay here's a check for your train fares.

Your uncle,
Emmet Whitney"

Mother let us look at the check, and Dan let out a war whoop and grabbed both her arms. "You'll say yes, won't you, Mother?" he asked breathlessly. "Can't we start the day after school closes—next week?"

"Now wait, we must think this over first." She looked at me. "Do you want to go too, Jack?"

"Of course!" I'd been thinking how I liked Uncle Emmet for writing "when" word came from Dad, instead of "if," even though I'd never seen him.

"Uncle Emmet is my closest relative," Mother said slowly. "I think Dad would like us to be with him while we're waiting to hear." She bit her lip; then went on. "When Dad returns it will probably be to a California port. We could get to him more quickly from Montana. It's much closer than Missouri."

"Then let's go!" Dan exclaimed, and I wanted to know how soon we could start.

Mother hesitated and tapped the letter up and down on her hand. She said it would take a little time to close the house and get someone to water the garden and lawn—*if* she decided to go.

She stood up. "I'm going to telephone Van Burden and see what he thinks about this."

Mr. Burden was Dad's boss. He was the editor of the newspaper that had sent Dad to Korea. It was hard for us to keep quiet while Mother was on the phone, but we could tell right away that Mr. Burden liked the idea, because Mother kept saying things like, "You really think it's a good idea?" and, "Yes, I know it will be cooler in Montana."

I was wondering what the ranch would look like and

whether Uncle Emmet would have some horses we could ride when I heard Mother say, "But— Oh, Van —it's such a wild country. And the boys are so young."

Dan and I looked at each other and knew why Mother hadn't been able to make up her mind. She was afraid we'd get thrown or kicked by a horse, or fall off a cliff or something. I was twelve and Dan was ten, and we were both tall for our age, but Mother still thought we were little kids. So we were surprised when she turned away from the phone a few minutes later and said, "Well, boys, I've decided to go."

Now that everything was settled we got so excited we were both talking at once. It was almost like Christmas Eve, when you knew something wonderful was going to happen and could hardly wait until morning. It even seemed as if Dad wasn't missing, but just away in Korea, as he'd been for over a year.

We got Mother to tell us again how Uncle Emmet ran away from home when he was fourteen because he couldn't get along with his stepmother; how he rode a freight train to Montana, and didn't have a cent, or any warm clothes when he got there; and how a kind rancher gave him a job herding sheep, and, when times got bad, paid him off in orphan lambs and gave him his start in the sheep business. Now Uncle Emmet owned a big ranch, called the Rising Arrow, that had six thousand sheep and was near Yellowstone National Park.

It seemed like a fairy story, and I said so. Mother smiled. "You mustn't get any false ideas. Uncle Emmet's a queer old codger. He's never married. He never liked women—because of his stepmother, I suppose. He won't even have a woman on the place. I'm surprised he's willing to put up with me for the summer."

"But you're different," we both said at once.

"Let's hope Uncle Emmet will think so. He hasn't seen me since I was a child." Mother looked sober, and I knew she was thinking how it would be if we got up there, so far from home, and didn't like it.

But Dan and I *knew* we would like it and wanted her to telephone Uncle Emmet right away so she couldn't change her mind. But she waited until night to telephone him that we were coming, and the very next week we boarded the train for Montana.

2. A Hair-raising Ride

Uncle Emmet had told Mother he'd meet us at White-hall, a town fifty miles from his ranch. We woke up early the morning we were to arrive. Dan jerked up the shade on the window of our berth, and we both gasped. It was snowing! Snowing in June! Great, feathery flakes danced against the train window—flakes so thick that we could scarcely see the outlines of the tall, dark mountains beyond.

We hurried, all excited, into our clothes, and rushed down the aisle to Mother's berth. It was plain to see that she didn't share our pleasure. She said, "Oh, no!" and raised the shade; and her eyes grew big and dark, the way they'd been the time Dan broke his leg. I suddenly remembered a book I'd read about a Canadian family getting lost in a snowstorm and almost perishing.

"Is it a blizzard?" I asked, trying to keep my voice from sounding as if I were scared.

"Of course not!" She tousled my hair, but her smile was a little shaky.

"Suppose Uncle Emmet can't meet us?" Dan must have remembered the book too.

"Now don't borrow trouble," Mother said briskly. "Go to the diner and order your breakfast. I'll come as soon as I'm dressed."

But Dan was right. When we got off at Whitehall two hours later nobody was in sight but a man in overalls who was pushing a mail truck.

The snow was coming down faster now. It feathered our coats and hats, and we could hardly see the line of stores across from the depot.

Mother peered down the street through the curtain of snow. "I suppose Uncle Emmet was delayed by the storm," she said after a minute. "I think I see a hotel. We'd better go there and wait until we hear from him."

We picked up our bags and began to walk down the platform. Nobody said anything, but we all felt let down, and I could tell that Mother was upset. But she needn't have been, for just as we reached the depot a mud-splashed sedan rattled up to the curb and a wiry little man with a mustache hopped out and trotted toward us.

"The boss sent me for you," he said and reached for the suitcase Mother was carrying. But Mother hung on to it. She looked at the battered sedan, then back at the little man, and said stiffly, "I'm Mrs. Paul Graham, and these are my sons, Jack and Dan. You haven't told us who you are."

He pushed back his hat. His face was serious, but his mustache twitched. "I'm Mort Baker, the boss's camp tender. Look, ma'am, I ain't tryin' to kidnap you." With that he rubbed mud from the car door with a canvas-gloved hand. Mother got red in the face when she saw RISING ARROW printed there in big black letters.

He picked up Mother's hatbox now and looked it over with such an odd expression on his face that I wished Mother hadn't brought it. Mother didn't notice. She brushed some snow from her sleeve and asked nervously, "Do you think it's safe to start out in this storm?"

The little man's mustache twitched again. "This ain't no storm," he said in a choked voice. " 'Tain't nothin' but a little skiff of snow. It'll be gone by mid-afternoon." He stacked our luggage in the back end of the car; then he opened the front door for Mother.

"How far is Virginia City from the ranch?" she asked as she settled herself on the seat.

"Twelve miles."

"Why didn't you meet us there?"

"No railroad closer'n Whitehall." He started the engine and shifted gears.

We rolled out of Whitehall and down a long stretch of road. The snow began to thin before we'd gone far, but there wasn't much to see until we made a sharp turn and the car began to climb into mountains. They looked like the Missouri Ozarks, except there weren't any trees on them—just brown grass and cliffs of rock.

I leaned over. "How high are these mountains, Mr. Baker?"

He turned his head and grinned. "Better call me Mort. I ain't used to a handle on my name. And these ain't mountains, they're foothills." He snorted. "We won't hit real mountains this side of Virginia City." But he told us we'd climb to seventy-five hundred feet after we left that town.

We came out on a flat now and drove for quite a while over open country. Presently it stopped snowing and we could see huge, white-capped mountains in the distance. We drove and drove, and it seemed as if we never came any closer to the mountains. The sun was shining when we reached a little town called Sheridan, and we stopped there for lunch. We got a little better acquainted with our driver in the restaurant, and began to ask him questions as soon as we were on the road again. First I wanted to know what a camp tender was.

He grinned. "Nursemaid to a bunch of herders." Then he explained that the sheep weren't kept close to the Rising Arrow ranch house, as we'd thought, but up in the mountains, some distance away. The herders lived in covered wagons, he said, and it was his job to keep them supplied with groceries. "I got to move their wagons too—'bout once a month—so's the sheep won't overgraze the range."

"How many herders has Uncle Emmet got?"

"Four."

"Only four, for six thousand sheep?"

"Sure. One herder can handle two thousand easy— if his dogs are worth their keep—not countin' the lambs."

"Why don't you count the lambs?" Dan wanted to know.

"Because they ain't 'round long enough. They're born in May and shipped in September. Boss only keeps enough ewe lambs to make up the winter's loss. They—"

He broke off suddenly and pulled the car to the side

of the road in front of an old two-storied log house with a balcony across it. "That's Robbers' Roost, boys," Mort said. "Used to be a stage stop in the gold-rush days. Road agents hung out there by the dozen and robbed and killed many a stage passenger that had made his stake and was headin' home with it."

Road agents! Gold rush! Dan and I stared for a minute; then we begged to get out and see what the log house was like inside. Mort said he couldn't take the time because he had to move a camp after he got back to the ranch. But I guess he felt sorry that we were so disappointed, because he told us a lot about road agents as we drove on. He said they had been in cahoots with Plummer.

"Who's he?" I asked.

"Ain't you never heard of Plummer?" Mort turned halfway around in his seat and squinted at us. Before we could answer, the car hit a shoulder and skidded off the road in a shower of gravel. Mother gasped, and told us to sit right back in our seats and stop bothering Mort with our questions.

"Oh, they ain't botherin' me none," Mort said, not taking the hint. He told us that Plummer had been the sheriff in the Alder Gulch gold-rush days. "Sheriff, and boss of the road agents too. Only folks didn't know it. So Plummer'd mooch around and find out when a shipment of gold dust was leavin', and then he'd light out and tip off his pals. That bunch got away with a sight of gold dust and nuggets before the vigilantes caught on to Plummer's tricks and hanged the whole gang."

Even Mother was interested now. I guess that was because we'd hit a straight piece of road. Mort gestured ahead in the direction of Virginia City and kept one hand on the steering wheel.

"Who discovered the gold?" Mother asked.

"Man name of Fairweather—and 'twas just an accident he did. Fairweather and some of his pals stopped in a gulch ten miles ahead to rest their horses. It was noon and they was hungry, and there wasn't no way to get grub because the Crow Indians'd stole all their rifles a few days before. Fairweather went across the creek to tether the ponies and happened to see a piece of rimrock. He called to a man named Edgar to bring him a pick and a pan. The two men dug in the grass and washed out a full pan of pay dirt.

"They hit it so rich that next day they lit out for Bannock to get a grub stake. Word got noised around, and the gold rush was on. When they started back, three hundred people followed them to stake out claims. They named the settlement at the head of the gulch Virginia City. In two years that little scoop in the mountains had a population of ten thousand, and later 'most three times that. 'Twas the state capital for a while."

"I should think a town that large would have a railroad," Mother said.

Mort chuckled. "Bet there ain't five hundred people live there now—in winter, that is. Summer, tourists come through in droves."

He told us that Virginia City had been almost a ghost town until twelve or fifteen years before, when a man named Bovee decided to patch up a few of the old buildings and got so interested that he restored most of the town.

"You ought to get the boss to bring you over sometime," Mort said. "You never seen anything like it. That feller Bovee must've ransacked every old attic in Montana. Anyway, now he's got all the buildings furnished just like they was in Plummer's day."

Mort rolled a cigarette with his free hand, put it between his lips, and struck a match with his thumbnail. Then he took a puff and went on talking. "If the boss brings you over to Virginia City you'll see Boot Hill too, where Clubfoot George and a lot more road agents is buried." Mort grinned and looked slyly at Mother. "They got George's foot, big as life, pickled in the museum—with a piece of his sock still hangin' to it."

"How awful!" Mother exclaimed.

"No, ma'am. There was a reason for it. You see, when the vigilantes jerked the ropes off the road agents' necks and buried them they wasn't in no mood for a fancy funeral. They just sorta chucked them in the ground helter-skelter, trustin' their memories as to which was which. Later, when folks cooled off some and decided to mark the graves better, nobody could agree on two of them, George's and one other feller's. So they just dug them up to make sure."

"And put that—that *thing* in the museum," Mother said chokingly, "for little children to see!"

"Guess they figured it wouldn't hurt kids none to find out that crime don't pay." Mort winked at us.

The road was beginning to get narrow and full of curves, so Mort didn't have much to say for a while. We'd been passing mound after mound of gravel, which lined the right side of the road, and finally Dan said, "What funny-looking hills!"

"You're in Alder Gulch now," Mort told us. "Those diggin's was left by the dredges. After the gold played out, somebody back East dredged millions of dollars from that gravel—dredged up some Montana rubies and garnets too. Once I run on to a ten-carat ruby."

I could tell that Mother didn't believe that, but Mort dug into his pocket and brought out a little chamois bag. He told Mother to look inside, and even she was impressed when she saw the ring. It had a beautiful red stone that sparkled in the sunlight. Dan and I were so excited we could hardly sit still. We begged Mort to stop and let us look for rubies, but he said we were running late and that we'd have to get Uncle Emmet to bring us back some other time.

We followed those gravel mounds all the way into Virginia City. The main street looked just like pictures we'd seen of early-day mining camps. Mort pointed out the old state capitol—a plain, square, brick building that didn't look anything like our capitol in Missouri—a frame building where six road agents were hung in one day; Boot Hill; and the museum. When he stopped in front of the post office for a minute and went in for the mail, we spotted a stagecoach standing in front of a store.

"Do you suppose they still use those here?" I asked Mother.

Mother smiled. "For local color perhaps."

"I'm going to ask Mort," Dan said.

"For goodness' sake, don't get him to talking again. I'd feel a lot safer if he just attended to his driving when we start over that mountain."

We looked and decided she was right, for the winding road that climbed the mountain ahead seemed to hang onto the very edge.

3. Uncle Emmet's Ranch

The trip over the mountain into the valley is something I'll never forget. Neither Dan nor I had ever seen high mountains until our train came through Wyoming the day before. We found that looking at them from a train window and driving over them isn't the same at all.

We climbed for seven miles, and Mort took the hairpin curves, it seemed to us, on two wheels. Mother got white about the mouth, and Dan and I huddled together, expecting the car to hurtle over the side and into the ravine below at any minute.

Actually, we discovered later, Mort was a skillful driver, and the road wasn't as dangerous as it appeared to our inexperienced eyes. Dan and I were ashamed of our fright and never admitted it, except to each other, but from that day on Mother would never ride in any car that Mort was driving.

Halfway to the top of the mountain my ears began to pop and feel queer. I kept pulling at them and rubbing them, until finally Mother turned and asked me what was wrong.

"My ears feel funny," I said.

Mort laughed. "It's the altitude. We're climbing fast now. You just swaller and the popping'll stop."

But Mort stopped first—on top of the mountain—to point out the valley that spread below and a river he said was the Madison. The river looked like a shining silver ribbon rippling through the valley, but I guess none of us appreciated it that day. We were too busy looking at the road that wound down like a snake to level ground and wondering if we'd get there alive.

Mother closed her eyes when we started again, and Dan and I sat very still and gazed at the back of Mort's neck. When we finally got to the bottom Mort turned and looked at us. "Well, I'll say this for you, you never let out a peep. Most greenhorns'd be howling still."

He didn't know that there wasn't enough breath left in us to let out a peep.

We turned off now on a graveled road that followed the Madison River as far as we could see. It was a wide, shallow river and full of boulders. The water was as clear as crystal, and so swift that it foamed and boiled over the rocks.

"Bet you never saw a river before that froze from the bottom up in winter," Mort said boastfully. "Ain't but one other in the world, they say, and that's in the old country."

He explained that this happened because slush ice

formed on the surface of the river, sank to the bottom, and clung to the boulders; then, little by little, the ice built up until it sometimes gorged.

He said a gorge was formed by little, jagged mountains of ice that collect and dam the channel of a stream on a bend or near a bridge, backing up the water until it breaks away and sometimes floods the whole countryside.

While Mort talked he kept gesturing back over his shoulder toward islands where, he said, cattle and horses and sheep had been trapped by a gorge and drowned. I could see that Mother was getting fidgety again. She showed it so plainly I was afraid she'd hurt his feelings, but suddenly he broke off in the middle of a story and pointed ahead.

"There's the lower end of the Rising Arrow," he said. "It runs fifteen miles upcountry from there, into the mountains. How's that for a ranch?"

A few minutes later he slid the car to a stop in front of a big log gate. A weatherbeaten sign swung above it. The lettering was faint, but I made out the words "Rising Arrow" and, just below, a brand that looked like this: ↑

"One of you kids hop out and open the gate," Mort said.

Both of us jumped out, glad to stretch our legs. We looked all around us, but couldn't see a sign of a house, a barn, or a corral. Ahead of us lay only more foothills, and beyond them high, timbered mountains, with patches of snow on their peaks.

"Where's the house?" I asked as we climbed back into the car.

"In a canyon three miles upcountry," Mort said.

"That's a queer place to build a house." Mother looked disappointed, because she loves a view.

"Not hereabouts. Most ranchers build where they'll be sheltered from some of the wind and snow."

"When will we see the sheep?" Dan wanted to know.

Mort laughed. "Told you they wasn't going to be hanging 'round the back door. They're up on the range."

The car climbed through a narrow draw and came out on a huge flat that stretched toward the mountains. The flat seemed to be a field of some kind. It was faintly green, the first green we'd seen since we left Whitehall.

Mort gestured. "Alfalfa and grain fields. Injuns used to hunt all over this country. When the boss first plowed this ground we found more arrowheads than we could count."

"Honest?" Dan was hanging over the front seat again. "You're not fooling us, Mort?"

"I sure ain't. See that red bluff over there? That's where the Injuns camped and chipped out arrowheads and spearheads. Obsidian, they was."

"What's obsidian?" I asked.

"Black rock. Looks like glass. The tribes'd bring it from the Yellowstone Park country in chunks, and while they hunted the squaws holed up under that bluff and chipped out their ammunition. There's still chunks of obsidian and broken arrowheads there."

He told us that the creek that ran through the canyon was called Wigwam Creek, because the Indians always used to camp there on hunting expeditions.

"There's a cave up near the beaver dams where they made their traps in bad weather."

"How do you know all this?" Mother asked suspiciously. "That must have been almost a century ago."

"Easy to figger out, ma'am. The walls of the cave're smoked black from their fires. And once when I was nosin' 'round I run across a few thongs of shriveled-up leather they used to make traps with. That, and bein' so close to the beaver dams, shows what they was up to."

He pointed down the canyon. "They say there's a cliff over there that was once a Injun buffalo-jump. Injuns used to slaughter hundreds of buffaloes by driving them over the top of a steep cliff. I always meant to go down-canyon and nose 'round, but I never got the time for it."

"Will you take us sometime?" Dan was squirming with excitement.

I was glad I hadn't asked, because Mort snorted and said, "What's wrong with you going by yourselves? Young fellers, if you got any idea you're going to be wet-nursed on this ranch you can get it right out of your heads."

We'd come to the gap that was the canyon now. We zipped down a steep grade, catching only a glimpse of some log buildings half hidden by huge cottonwood trees before we reached the bottom. We rolled over a cattle guard, through a barnyard, and over a bridge that spanned a swift little creek. The car drew up before a great two-storied log house, and Mort pushed back his hat and said, "This is it, kids. Shake a leg and help me wrangle your bags into the house."

4. Uncle Emmet and Molly

As we started up the board walk to the house we heard a furious barking inside. The door opened, and a fat old black-and-white shepherd dog burst through it, followed by a giant of a man. I'll never forget my first sight of Uncle Emmet. Mother had said he was a big man, but I guess she must have forgotten how big. All of him was big. I noticed his hands first. They were huge. Once I'd seen a strong man in a circus straighten an iron hoop into a bar with his bare hands. Dad told me at the time that it was a trick, that he couldn't possibly have done it, but I remember thinking when I first saw Uncle Emmet that he might *really* be able to do it.

The next thing I noticed was a shock of gray hair above a face as brown as leather and lots younger than I'd expected it to be. The only wrinkles I could see were laugh wrinkles around his mouth, just like Dad's. He had on a plaid shirt, a fringed leather jacket, levis, and fancy boots.

I might have stood there gaping a lot longer if Mother hadn't called out, "Uncle Emmet!" and started running to meet him. The minute she did the old dog headed her off, growling horribly, the fur standing straight up on its back.

Mother shrieked, and got back through the gate in a hurry, pulling Dan and me with her. Shaking all over, she slammed the gate and warned, "Don't get near that animal! It's vicious."

Uncle Emmet shouted, "Molly!" and the dog, to our surprise, slunk meekly to his heels and lay down. Uncle Emmet opened the gate and shook hands with

Mother—this rather surprised her, I guess, because she'd held up her face for a kiss—and after that he shook hands with Dan and me. All the time Mother was eying the old dog and still hanging on to us. I wished she wouldn't. I didn't want Uncle Emmet to get the idea we were a couple of babies.

"Well, let's go inside," Uncle Emmet said.

Mother hung back and said nervously, "Can't you tie that dog up? I'm afraid she'll bite the boys."

Uncle Emmet threw back his big head and shouted with laughter. " 'Tain't the boys she's making such a fuss about, Niece. It's you. She don't like women. But we'll settle this right now. Molly!" he boomed. "Come here!"

The dog slunk up on her belly. "Now mind your manners," Uncle Emmet said softly. "This woman here's my kin. Give her a paw."

Immediately the dog sat down and lifted a paw. Mother put out her hand. She didn't trust Molly, but she was game. And Molly *did* mind her manners, for when Uncle Emmet led us into a huge dining room she waddled along beside Mother as peaceably as you please.

The dining room had a checked-oilcloth-covered table that ran the full length of the room, with benches the same length on either side of it. There was an enormous potbellied stove that reached halfway to the ceiling at the far end of the room. The stove had an isinglass door and a lot of fancy nickel trimmings.

But the thing that fascinated me the most was a string of moose, bear, and antelope heads that hung clear around the wall. They were glassy-eyed and snarling, and they looked so real and ferocious that they took my breath away for a minute. Mother's too, I guess. She was staring at them, and she looked as if she were going to cry. I knew she was thinking of our safe dining room in Springfield, with its pretty round table and ladder-back chairs and the big window where her flowers bloomed the year round.

And then the strangest thing happened. Molly waddled over to her, jumped up, licked her hand, and began to whine friendly little whines.

Mother got down on her knees and hugged the old dog. "Oh, Molly," she said, "I do believe you like me after all."

"Derned if I don't think she does too." Uncle Emmet scratched his head. He had the queerest look on his face, and I got the idea he hadn't meant for Molly to love Mother, but just not to growl at her any more. I wanted to laugh. Somebody in the kitchen did snicker.

"Bastian!" Uncle Emmet shouted, and a fat little man with an apron around his middle slouched through the door and eyed us curiously. While he was looking, one of his eyes seemed to wander off to the side, so it looked as if he were taking us all in at the same time. I couldn't tell whether he was looking at Mother and me, or Dan, who was on the other side of the room.

"Bastian," Uncle Emmet said, "this is my niece and her boys. Now hustle and bring us some coffee."

"None for the boys," Mother said firmly.

"Rats! Coffee never hurt anybody. It'll put hair on their chests."

Mother didn't say anything. I guess she decided not to argue with Uncle Emmet on our very first day. She never did have to argue about coffee because, when Bastian brought it, in heavy white mugs with no handles, we didn't like it. It was as strong as lye and kind of thick and bitter. Later on I found out why. Bastian kept putting fresh grounds in with the old grounds, until the pot wouldn't hold any more. Then he'd throw it out and start all over again.

"Sorry I couldn't meet you," Uncle Emmet apologized after he'd emptied a cup of coffee. "Had a pile-up in a gully near the shearing pens this morning. We're shorthanded, and I had to skin out the dead."

Mother must have remembered Clubfoot George's pickled foot, for she caught her breath and stammered, "Dead—w-what?"

"Sheep." Uncle Emmet shook with laughter. "Did you think it was men?"

Mother looked embarrassed. "I guess you'll think

we're green until we get on to Montana talk. Just what is a pile-up?"

Right away I could tell that Uncle Emmet liked to talk about his sheep, even when something bad had happened to them. He said pile-ups occurred because sheep had a habit of following one another blindly.

"It's like this," he said. "If a lead sheep runs into a snowbank, a fence, or anything he can't get over in a hurry, he's in trouble, because the rest of the herd keep right on coming and trample him under. They get so much pressure from the sheep behind they can't stop, so they fall over one another and then you have a pile-up."

He told us that a pile-up was one of the most dreaded of calamities on a sheep ranch because sheep smother quickly, and sometimes hundreds of sheep could die in a very few minutes if there wasn't a herder nearby to separate them.

"I've always heard that sheep dogs are intelligent," Mother said. "Couldn't they do something about it?"

Uncle Emmet shook his head. "Nothing but bark and snap, and that just rattles the sheep worse."

Old Molly waddled over and put her head against Mother's knee, and Uncle Emmet scratched his head again and looked like he couldn't believe what he saw.

"Is Molly a sheep dog?" Mother asked, stroking the dog's shaggy back.

"She's a retired sheep dog," Uncle Emmet said. "When they get too old to work we bring them down to the house. But Molly's been a top sheep dog in her day. She's earned her keep a thousand times over. Someday I'll tell you about how she saved a whole flock of sheep in a blizzard."

"Tell us now," I begged, eying Molly with new respect.

"No. Not now." Uncle Emmet pushed back his chair. "You boys got any levis?"

We nodded.

"Well, get out of those dude clothes and I'll show you some of your chores." He scowled, and his bushy brows made little tents over his eyes, which were very blue and twinkling, in spite of the scowl. "You got to earn your keep if you stay around here. Everybody works on this ranch." Then he looked at Mother and grinned. "I'm fixing to put some muscle and tallow on these kids," he said, "so's their pa won't think he's borned a couple of scarecrows when he gets home."

Dan and I didn't think we were especially skinny, and we were afraid Uncle Emmet meant to say "sissies." If Mother just wouldn't always be so afraid we were going to get hurt! The minute we got off alone I was going to ask her not to let on in front of the men how she worried about us. I even felt a little cross with her.

But just then Mother laughed. It was the first time she'd really laughed as if she meant it since the telegram from the Defense Department had come. It made me feel good, so good I didn't mind Uncle Emmet's teasing any more.

5. Thunder and Lightning

As we started upstairs to change clothes Uncle Emmet told us to take any room we wanted except the one that had a door into the bathroom, which was to be Mother's. The rooms, four of them, looked exactly alike. Each had a bed, a chair, and a chest of drawers. Mother's room had a little mirror hanging over the chest. It was new, and we grinned at each other when we saw it. Uncle Emmet had made one concession to a woman guest after all. It was plain we were expected to use the tin basin and mirror we'd seen in the kitchen.

We picked the room over the kitchen—one with a big dinner-bell post just outside the window—and got into our levis double quick. But Uncle Emmet was shouting, "Shake a leg, boys!" before we were ready. When we finally raced downstairs he looked us over from head to foot.

"Tennis shoes!" he exploded. "Whoever heard of ranching in tennis shoes? Ain't you got any boots?"

We shook our heads. It seemed as if we'd never be

able to measure up to the Rising Arrow. We knew Mother couldn't afford to buy us expensive boots and expected to be ashamed of our feet the rest of the summer. But we didn't know Uncle Emmet well then.

"What size shoes do they wear?" he asked Mother.

She told him, and he wrote it down in a little black book. Then he said, "Well, we'll fix that right quick. Mort's hauling salt from Virginia City tomorrow. I'll have him bring some boots back."

Mother said he oughtn't to go to that expense; that we couldn't wear boots out in a summer and they'd be outgrown before we could use them again. I held my breath for fear Uncle Emmet would agree.

But he said, "If I know boys they'll be in shreds by haying time. Besides, I don't want them crippled by stone bruises. They've got work to do around here." He grabbed his hat. "Come along, fellows!"

We followed him down the path from the house, over the swift little creek that was green with watercress, and into the corral. We were so happy over the promised boots it was all we could do to keep from running and shouting. But when we got to the corral we forgot the boots and everything else.

Uncle Emmet put a big hand on my shoulder and another on Dan's. "See those ponies?" He nodded toward two horses, a black and a roan, which were drinking at the creek that ran through the corral.

They were beautiful horses, sleek and full of spirit,

for they tossed their heads as they took us in, and one of them pawed the earth. For just a moment I thought he was going to tell us we could ride them for the summer, but then I saw two other horses behind them, dozing in the sun. Both were sway-backed, and they looked old and gentle. I was sure those were the horses he meant us to ride, if we rode at all, and I was so disappointed I couldn't say a word.

Uncle Emmet's hand bore down on my shoulder. "Cat got your tongue?" he asked gruffly. "Don't you like the looks of those ponies? Because if you don't, it's too bad. They're yours."

I gulped, and Dan stood there with his jaw hanging down. We couldn't believe it was true until Uncle Emmet said, "They're yours. And just so there'll be no squabbling and choosing, I'm giving the black to you, Dan, and the roan to Jack. You got to take care of them, and if I ever catch you neglecting them, back to the range they'll go."

We found our voices then and both of us shouted, "We'll take care of them!" I wanted to hug Uncle Emmet, but somehow I knew he wouldn't like that, so I just said, "Thank you!" Dan did too, and he caught Uncle Emmet's arm and asked if we could catch them right away.

"If that ain't just like a tenderfoot." Uncle Emmet chuckled. "A fat chance you'd have catching those horses. They've been kicking up their heels on the range all winter. You got to outfox them. Just wait till I get some oats."

The minute he came out of the barn shaking two cans of oats both ponies jerked up their heads and came racing toward us. We fed them and petted them while they were eating. They had the ⚡ brand on their left shoulder, and Uncle Emmet told us it was a very old horse brand. Years before he had bought the ranch an Englishman owned the lower grazing land. He raised and broke horses to be used in the Boer War, and it was he who had named the ranch after the brand.

When the horses finished their oats I asked if we couldn't saddle and ride them.

Uncle Emmet said, "Not in those dude shoes. Wait till tomorrow." But he let us curry them until their coats shone, and he let us name them. Dan called his black "Thunder," and I named the roan "Lightning." Weeks later we learned that they'd been called Bud and Joe before we got them but by that time we'd also learned that Uncle Emmet, for all his gruffness, was the kindest person in the world and wouldn't take the shine off his gifts by telling us the horses already had names.

While we were currying the ponies Uncle Emmet pitched hay down from the haymow for the other horses. There were four others: Uncle Emmet's big gray, Duke; Mort's chestnut, Sally; and the two older horses, Dolly and Blue. Dolly and Blue were the horses Mort used for packing supplies into the mountains over roads that were too steep and rough for the trucks or buckboard to travel. Uncle Emmet said pack horses had to be gentle and willing to go anywhere they were led.

We weren't very interested in Dolly and Blue that afternoon and would much rather have talked about our own ponies. But there came a time, a few months later, when we were mighty glad we knew that pack horses were especially trained.

When Uncle Emmet finished pitching hay he put the fork back in the big barn and said it was time to go back to the house and wash up before supper. The bell rang just as we crossed the creek. We thought we were late, but our uncle said that it was only the "wash-up" bell, which Bastian always rang fifteen minutes ahead of a meal.

I'd been wishing there was some way we could show Uncle Emmet how grateful we were. As we went through the gate I remembered what he'd said about earning our keep. "Will you put us to work tomorrow?" I asked.

He looked pleased and put an arm across my shoulders. "I got a big job for you boys," he said, "and it'll last right up till haying." He said the job was poisoning gophers, and explained that gophers destroyed more feed than we could ever imagine. "There's one to every square foot in the alfalfa and grain fields and they're multiplying every day." Then he told us that we'd have to find their holes and sprinkle poisoned oats nearby.

"Can we ride Thunder and Lightning to the field?" Dan asked eagerly.

"Not on your life! You want to get those ponies poisoned right off? Anyhow, you couldn't ride a horse and carry a rifle, and you'll need a gun to pick off stray gophers. Ever used a gun?" He squinted at us.

We had to admit that we hadn't, but we didn't tell him that Mother had never even let us own a BB gun.

"Well, it won't take long to learn. We'll set up some targets after supper."

Now we were really excited. "Do you suppose Mother will let us?" Dan whispered as we dashed up the stairs.

"Let's wait and let Uncle Emmet bring up the subject," I whispered back, remembering what good luck he'd had with the coffee.

So when we burst into her room to tell her about Thunder and Lightning we didn't mention guns; and it was just as well, because she said right away, "I hope they're old, gentle horses."

Down in the dining room Uncle Emmet introduced us to two more of the ranch hands, men he called Shorty and Bill. He told us the rest of the home ranch crew had gone up to the shearing pens to get the place ready for shearing, and that the shearers would be there in another three days.

Bastian brought in a huge platter of fried ham, some baked potatoes and beans, vegetables, and thick slices of homemade bread. Before we finished supper we decided that Bastian might not know how to brew coffee but he could certainly cook. He was a great talker too and could tell the most exciting stories about things that had happened on the ranch. We soon learned that he knew almost everything and never looked scornful when we asked questions, as some of the men did. We asked a lot, after we got used to the way his eye sometimes slid off center.

That evening we finished our supper with great slabs of gooseberry pie, and as soon as we had stacked our dishes and taken them to the kitchen like the rest of the men Uncle Emmet went into his office, and came out with a .22-caliber rifle in his hand.

"Come on, boys," he said. "Let's get in some target practice before dark."

Dan nudged me, and I held my breath. It was just as we'd been afraid it would be. Mother jumped to her feet and said real quick, "No! I won't let them. They might have an accident. I wouldn't dare."

We looked at Uncle Emmet. He winked at us and took Mother's arm. "Niece Helen," he said, "it's time you and me had a little talk." With that he led her into his office and shut the door. We waited anxiously for fifteen minutes before they came out.

I don't know what Uncle Emmet said to Mother, but whatever it was he'd won her over. She still looked uncertain, but she said, "Your uncle thinks you're old enough to handle a gun. He thinks Dad would want you to—now that you have the chance. But, oh, boys, be careful."

She couldn't bring herself to watch us take our first lesson. She followed us outside, but when Uncle Emmet put a can on a gatepost and showed me how to hold and fire the rifle she slipped away.

I'm afraid neither Dan nor I came up to Uncle Emmet's expectations as marksmen. Dan managed to hit the can once at twenty feet, and I only grazed it. After a while Uncle Emmet said it was getting too dark to practice and he put the rifle away.

"Takes practice, boys," he said as we went back into the house. "Tell you what. The day you can hit the target four times out of six, I'll turn you loose on the gophers."

6. Dan and I Explore

The rising bell rang at five-thirty the next morning and we stumbled out of bed, half asleep, and hurried into our clothes. Then we ran down to the corral to pitch hay for Thunder and Lightning. Mother went with us. The ponies were full of life that morning. When we opened the gate they tossed their heads, kicked up their heels, and circled the corral in a high run.

We wished they hadn't, because Mother frowned and said, "They don't look safe to me." But when they settled down to their hay we persuaded her to come pet them, and then she felt a little better about it.

After breakfast Uncle Emmet loaded a great stack of tents and some cooking vessels that were almost as big as small tubs on a truck to take up to the shearing camp. The shearers, he told us, would sleep in the tents. We hung around until he had finished loading.

Then he said, "You fellows just nose around today and look the place over. Tomorrow I'll set you to poisoning gophers."

We decided to explore a long shed we'd seen down the canyon first. The shed was quite a distance from the house, and we had to go through a corral to reach it. When we stepped inside the gate our feet sank into a regular carpet of dry, finely powdered manure. It was an old corral, Bastian told us later. The Indians had kept their horses there.

It took both of us to push the big sliding door open, and the minute we did there was a wild whir of wings, and a gray cloud seemed to explode and soar over our heads. It startled us so for a moment that we froze to the spot. Then Dan laughed and said, "They're sparrows! Hundreds of them!" I laughed too, but it didn't seem funny when we discovered that some of the sparrows hadn't made their escape. They'd smashed into a crossbeam and fluttered to the floor. They were all dead when we went to examine them. We felt bad about this, and buried them in a hole we dug near the fence.

It was gloomy inside the shed, although patches of sunlight streamed through cracks in the log chinking, and it smelled musty and sour. We found out what caused this smell when, at the far end of the building, we came upon stack after stack of sheep pelts—the winter's loss, Uncle Emmet told us that night.

We climbed up a ladder into the loft and found it packed almost solid with sacks of cottonseed cake and bins of a powdery mixture, which we later discovered was ground alfalfa.

The cake reached almost to the rafters. We hoisted ourselves on top of the sacks, and were having a lot of fun jumping from one to another, when suddenly Dan let out a shriek, leaped, and threw himself against me so hard that we both went down on the sacks together. He pointed a shaking finger. "It ran between my legs!"

"*What?*"

"A rat as big as a cat! Look! There it is, making for that bin!"

I looked and saw a gray shape slither around a corner of the bin.

Dan scrambled to his feet. "Let's get out of here!"

"Shucks," I said, "a rat won't hurt you if you let it alone." But I wasn't too sure about this one.

Just then we heard a funny little squeaking in the rafters, and, looking up, we discovered what turned out to be the big rat's nest. It was made of feathers and bits of rag and straw and, when we got up the nerve to investigate, it turned out to be the queerest nest we'd ever seen. It was half full of shiny things: metal shavings, beer-bottle caps, several links of a gold chain, and a pair of cuff links with some kind of blue stone in them. But the most interesting things there were four piglike baby rats, pink and hairless and no bigger than my thumb.

"Let's take them back to the house and show Mother!" Dan exclaimed. "There's two apiece. Maybe she'll let us keep them for pets."

I didn't think we'd better take the rats, but we did take the cuff links. When we showed them to Bastian at noon he almost exploded. "I lost them a year back!" he exclaimed, and his bad eye seemed to go in every direction. "Thought they'd been stole!"

He told us we should have killed the baby rats, and said they were pack rats and would steal any shiny thing they came across, besides destroying a lot of cake and grain every year. "If you ever run onto one of their caches again you kill their young!" he warned.

We'd seen enough of the shed so now we went to the blacksmith shop, where Bill was shoeing Dolly, the old pack mare. He was just putting on the last shoe, and we were disappointed that we hadn't got there sooner. We watched him trim Dolly's hoof and pound the red-hot shoe on the anvil until it fit. He even let us work the bellows to the forge, and when he led Dolly away we were torn between following him to the barn and exploring the shop. We decided on the shop.

It was a fascinating place, and we stayed there almost an hour. The walls were crowded with traps of all sizes, guns with broken stocks or triggers, a hundred lanterns (we counted them), a lot of rattlesnake skins, and some queer contraptions we later discovered were used to stretch the skins of beaver, weasel, mink, and muskrat.

In one corner of the shed we found an emery wheel and had a lot of fun sharpening our pocket knives. There were rake and mowing-machine parts in another corner, and buckets of wagon grease, and several boxes marked "dynamite," and a coil of fuse. There was also a quart jar full to the top with rattlesnake rattles.

"Gosh!" Dan said, "I hope Mother never takes a notion to come in here. If she does she won't let us out of the house."

We went to the bunkhouse next. Four two-decker bunks lined one wall, and the mattresses on them were filled with straw. The stove had been made from a huge oil barrel, and a kettle of water was singing on top of it. All four of the bunks had rifles and six-shooters hanging from them in leather holsters that had been rubbed with some kind of oil until they shone. We pulled a .45 half out of its holster to look it over, then dropped it back gingerly.

There was a basin in one corner with a mirror above it and a stack of razors and shaving soap and brushes and mugs. Clothes were scattered all over the place— overalls, Pendleton pants, wool shirts, windbreakers, long wool socks, and chaps. Some of the chaps were very fancy, with silver conchos and colored stones trimming their belts. It was almost like looking at a Western movie, except there weren't any guitars or banjos in sight.

The dinner bell rang before we were half finished looking. Mother was shocked when we told her we'd been nosing around in the bunkhouse. "How would you like to have some stranger pawing all through your things?" she asked sternly.

But we didn't think the men would mind very much, since everything was right out in the open, and we were glad we'd gone in when we had because she forbade us to go there again unless we were invited.

After midday dinner Mother took a nap and we went down to the icehouse with Bastian. It was a log building too, and one side of it was partitioned off and filled with great chunks of ice buried in sawdust. On the other side half a side of beef, a sheep, and some dressed chickens were strung from the rafters. It was hard to believe that so much meat could be found any-where except in a butcher shop.

When I said so, Bastian shrugged and cocked one eye at me. "The shearers'd clean this up in four meals. They're going to butcher two more steers at the shearing pens tonight."

He shouldered the beef to the chopping block, sharpened a long knife on a whetstone, and cut and sawed off a roast for supper.

After that we followed him to the smokehouse. The smoke from a fire smoldering in the middle of the dirt floor belched out and stung our eyes and set us to coughing. Slab after slab of bacon, a lot of hams, and some link sausages hung down from the smoke-black-ened rafters, and some barrels filled with pickled pigs' feet and shanks stood against the wall. Bastian threw several black birch limbs on the fire, let it blaze up, and then banked it. By now he was choking too, and all three of us ducked out the door.

On the way back to the house he asked us if we'd like to sprout some spuds. We said yes, without the faintest idea of what we'd agreed to do. He led us to a root-cellar that was built just like a mine, with a long tunnel dug into the side of the canyon. It was black as pitch inside, and Bastian took a flashlight from his pocket and let us look around.

One side of the tunnel was solid with bins of rutabagas, turnips, carrots, pumpkins, and squash, and hanging from the wall above them were onions tied into big bunches.

The potatoes were in a little room at the very back of the shaft. There seemed to be a mountain of them, and they were covered with long white sprouts. Bastian said he'd already sprouted six sacks for the shearing pens and would need another six before shearing was over. He filled a sack for each of us, dragged them outside the cellar into the sun, and showed us how to cut the sprouts off without harming the potato. We sprouted potatoes the rest of the afternoon, but only finished one sack and part of another. It was a dull job, but we stuck to it until Mort drove in before supper with a load of sheep-salt he'd trucked from Virginia City.

He'd brought our boots. They were beautiful boots, brown with green and red stitching. We were so proud of them we put them on right away. When

Uncle Emmet saw them he grinned and slapped us on our backs. "Now you're beginning to look like ranchers," he said.

We'd only been on the ranch two days, but already both Dan and I knew that we wanted to be ranchers when we grew up. We talked it over before we went to sleep that night and decided that we'd do every job that Uncle Emmet or any of the men gave us as well as we possibly could, and learn everything we could learn about the operation of the ranch.

"If only Mother wouldn't be so scared over every little thing!" Dan sighed just before we dropped off to sleep.

7. Gophers

Next morning Uncle Emmet gave each of us a bucket of poisoned oats and sent us down to the field. He also gave us some canvas gloves and warned us to wear them and keep our hands away from our mouths.

"Put about a teaspoon of oats in the mouth of each hole," he said. "And after you've finished that job you can go over to where Shorty is irrigating and kill gophers when he drowns out their holes."

It didn't take us long to empty our buckets because there was a gopher hole almost everywhere we looked. We could see Shorty, in hip boots, with a shovel over his shoulder, at the far end of the field, so when we finished our job we ran over and told him what Uncle Emmet had said. He wasn't friendly the way Mort and Bastian and Bill were, and he told us gruffly to keep out of his way till he got a dam set.

The dams were just long strips of canvas with a pole nailed to one end. Small ditches ran all the way through the alfalfa and forked out from a main ditch that was much wider and deeper than the rest. When one portion of the field was flooded, Shorty set another canvas dam, then removed the first one. The water rushed down the big ditch until it was backed up by the second dam. As soon as it began to overflow into the small ditches Shorty called to us.

"Get off your boots and roll up your britches!" He gave us each a short piece of board and said, "You'll have to work fast to keep up with the water. The minute it floods their holes the gophers'll pop out and scatter. Whack them hard and make sure you kill them."

The water was freezing cold and the ground was so rocky it hurt our bare feet, but we had to move so fast we didn't notice after the first few minutes. I hated to kill the gophers. They looked so wet and pitiful as they popped out of their holes. I thought how I'd hate it if anyone flooded my home, and then I remembered what Uncle Emmet had said about the amount of grain they destroyed. After that I didn't mind as much.

At eleven o'clock we walked back to the house with Shorty and found out why he was in such a bad humor. He said every man on the ranch would be going up to the shearing pens the next day, which meant he would have to milk the cows and do all the chores that Bastian couldn't handle.

"Even you kids are going." He eyed us gloomily. "The boss's got you slated for water boys." This was wonderful news to us. We didn't know what water boys were, but we didn't care, so long as we got to go.

When we got back to the house Uncle Emmet was loading another truck to go to the shearing pens, this time with groceries from the cellar and hams and bacon from the smokehouse. The truck was already stacked with case after case of canned corn, tomatoes, pork and beans, hominy, and peas. We wanted to help Uncle Emmet but he said he was all finished, except for some hundred-pound sacks of sugar, flour, and coffee that would be too heavy for us to lift.

I'd never seen so much food in my life except in a grocery store. "How many men will be working at the shearing pens?" I wanted to know.

" 'Round thirty, counting shearers and herders and wranglers. Maybe more."

We trailed him back and forth from the cellar, and he told us there were sixteen shearers, including their captain, a Mexican named Alvarado. The crew started shearing in Arizona and New Mexico in January and worked through California, Nevada, Utah, and Idaho to Montana.

I asked him why Alvarado was called the captain, and he said every crew had to have a head man to bargain with ranchers in advance of the job. The shearers were paid by the number of sheep they sheared, and the captain got a certain percentage of each shearer's earnings.

"The captain's word is law. He can hire or fire. He can tongue-lash and use his fists too." Uncle Emmet chuckled as he hoisted a sack of sugar to his big shoulder. "Many's the time I've seen Alvarado knock a shearer flat on his back for nicking too many sheep with his blade shears."

He said nicking sheep was bad and a little of it couldn't be helped, but careless shearers sometimes cut chunks of flesh out along with the wool. Then flies would blow the open wound and maggots would kill the sheep.

When he had loaded the last sack and clamped down the end gates of the truck we asked him to let us go to the shearing pens with him after dinner. He said no, because he wouldn't be home until late.

"And I want you kids to get to bed early," he warned. "You'll see all the shearing you can stomach in the next few days. You're going to carry water for the crew, and we're setting out before daybreak in the morning."

We were so pleased to know that Shorty had told us the truth—we'd begun to think he hadn't until Uncle Emmet said so—that we didn't beg to go along any more.

That afternoon Mother and Dan and I sprouted potatoes for a while and then walked up the canyon to find the place where the squaws had made arrowheads. The brush and willows that followed the creek were so thick in places that Mother could scarcely get through, and we had to climb up and walk along the ridge so her skirt and stockings wouldn't get torn.

The red bluff of the canyon tilted over and sheltered a little clearing underneath. When we scrambled down the rocks we found it was just as Mort had said. There were dozens of broken or half-finished arrowheads and spearheads scattered over the ground, and some small chunks of obsidian too.

We picked up the best of the arrowheads and spearheads halfheartedly. What had seemed such an exciting adventure two days ago seemed tame today compared with the more exciting things going on at the ranch. We could hardly wait until the next day when we too would take a part in it.

8. A Visit to the Shearing Pens

It was dark and cold when Uncle Emmet awakened us
the next morning. We shivered as we got into our
clothes. This kind of weather in June seemed strange
to us—it had been hot for a month before we left
Springfield. We soon learned that it was always cold
in the early morning and late evening in Montana, but
it could get hot too, almost as hot as Missouri, in the
middle of the day and mid-afternoon. The heat was a
dry heat though, and you didn't feel it so much, and

the funny thing was that if you stepped into the shade, most times you didn't mind it at all.

Dan and I had known that the Rising Arrow was a big ranch but we never dreamed it was quite so big until that morning. We drove for twelve miles before we got to the shearing pens, and every mile was a part of the Rising Arrow property. The road was rocky and rough, and the truck climbed most of the time, until at last we came out on a big flat that was surrounded on all sides but one by low hills that hugged the timbered mountains beyond.

"Look, boys!" Uncle Emmet pointed. "There're the shearing pens."

We saw a long shed squatting in the middle of the flat. There were corrals on three sides of it, and beyond the shed a dozen or more tents. A little farther down the creek we could make out the roof of another building, half hidden by brush and trees. This was the cook shack, Uncle Emmet said.

Dan spotted a number of sheep on a hill, and as we came closer we saw sheep on three different hills, as well as a big bunch in one of the corrals. Uncle Emmet said they only brought one band down at a time so the ewes wouldn't have to leave their grazing or be separated from their lambs any longer than necessary.

We drove straight to the cook shack, where we had breakfast. The tables were even longer than those at the ranch house, and they were loaded with food—

stewed fruit, cereal, flapjacks, toast, both bacon and ham, and eggs. Two men cooks did the cooking and waited on the tables.

There wasn't much talk at the table. The men ate fast and a lot and drank cup after cup of coffee. Alvarado, a big-muscled, stern-looking man, sat at one end of the table and Uncle Emmet at the other. Alvarado only *looked* stern, we discovered later. He was really very friendly, and had the whitest teeth and the nicest smile I'd ever seen. Most of his crew had been with him for years, Uncle Emmet said, and they respected him because they knew he was just and honest and wouldn't stand for any careless shearing.

After breakfast we walked up to the shearing shed with Alvarado while Uncle Emmet stopped to talk with the cooks about the supplies they'd need the next day. We asked Alvarado so many questions on the way that he finally threw up his hands and said, "Look, muchachos, it'll be half an hour before the crew starts clipping so I'll just take you around and show you the setup."

He began with the pens. There were sixteen of them, and they were flanked on both sides by a long, narrow alleyway that ran the full length of the shed. There was a gate at one end which opened into a low-ceilinged, windowless lean-to. The lean-to was already packed tight with bleating ewes that were to be sheared that morning.

"The sweat shed," Alvarado told us.

It was still cool enough for our light denim jackets, but those sheep were panting and looked hot and miserable. Alvarado said that was good, because the grease from their bodies would penetrate the wool and make shearing easier.

"Makes the wool heavier too." He grinned. "And that won't hurt your uncle's feelings when he sells."

He said the sheep would be wrangled out of the sweat shed into the alleyway at the right, and from there, in small bunches, into the pens.

At the other end of the same alleyway another gate opened into a chute. This was the branding chute, and as soon as the ewes were sheared they'd be herded single file into the narrow passage to be branded and have their cuts doctored with sheep dip.

We were surprised to learn that the sheep were branded with waterproof paint and that each band had a separate brand. Alvarado got an envelope out of his pocket and marked down the brands for us. They were: ⊙ ◇ W ϛ

From the branding chute the sheep would be turned into a corral to wait until the whole band had been sheared, Alvarado told us. Then they'd be corralled with their lambs to "mother-up."

"I'm not going to tell you about 'mothering-up,'" he said. "It's something you'll want to see for yourselves. It's like nothing you've ever seen. You come back here and watch it after this band's sheared out."

We walked around the end of the pens to the other side. In the middle of the alleyway he pointed out an elevated platform from which a long wool sack hung. It was secured at the top by an iron hoop and its bottom cleared the floor by a foot.

Alvarado told us that as each fleece was sheared it was shoved out into the alleyway, where a man tied it into a tight bundle, and then pitched it up to another man who dumped it into the sack and tramped it down.

This man was called the "tromper," and Alvarado said the tromper had the dirtiest, most disagreeable job in the whole outfit. He had to get into the sack and stomp the wool down. He never got his head over the top until the sack was full, and by then he was almost smothered by heat and dust.

"He gets more pay than the wranglers, but there's not a man would change jobs with him. He's got to tramp between three hundred and fifty to four hundred pounds of wool into that sack before he can climb out." Alvarado laughed and pointed out a big man lounging against one of the pens. "There's the tromper. Better get a good look at him now. You won't know him in another hour."

While Alvarado had been taking us around, the

shearers had come in one by one. They all put an edge on their shears at an emery wheel near the door; then they took their places in the separate pens. When the wranglers started back to the sweat shed Alvarado said he'd have to leave us to shift for ourselves.

We hunted up Uncle Emmet and asked him to show us what we were supposed to do. He gave each of us a big bucket and told us the spring was downhill on the other side of the tents. "Now all you got to do is keep these buckets full of cold water and be ready to jump when somebody calls for a drink," he said.

It didn't seem like much of a job, and I guess he could see we were disappointed, because he laughed. "It's a bigger job than you think. You'll be dragging your feet this afternoon when it gets real hot and the crew gets dry."

He told the truth. We almost ran our legs off that afternoon, and by quitting time the little hill up from the spring seemed like a huge mountain before we got to the top with our last brimming buckets.

We had only a few calls for water before eleven o'clock, and we were glad because we were so interested in the shearing. It was fascinating to watch. A shearer would grab a ewe and throw her. As he balanced her body against his, his shears would skim through the wool. The fleece came off all in one piece, like a carpet, even and smooth. What surprised us most was how little the ewes struggled. They even seemed to like it. One old ewe closed her eyes and looked as if she were sleeping.

"She didn't mind a bit," I said to the shearer as he shoved her fleece into the aisle.

He grinned, "Muchacho, how you like winter overcoat on hot June day? You like to take off, no?"

But he said the band they were shearing was made up of old ewes that had been sheared before and that the two-year-old ewes, sheared for the first time, put up quite a fight.

Just then I heard someone shouting angrily and looked around to see two men, one of them a shearer, arguing over some figures marked on a card that was tacked to a post. A sudden hush fell over the shed. The blades all down the line of pens stopped in mid-air as the argument grew louder and hotter.

I'd been wondering what those cards were—one in front of each pen—and now I found out. They were the only record kept of the number of sheep clipped by a shearer, and the figures were marked down by a man called a tallyer as the sheared ewes were turned into the alleyway.

The tallyer was red in the face, and he kept shouting that the count was right. The shearer was waving his arms wildly and claiming it was wrong. He shouted some words in Spanish, and I know they must have been cuss words because the tallyer smashed him in the face with his fist. They went down together, and rolled over and over on the board floor.

The rest of the shearers leaped to their feet to watch the fight. The wranglers came tearing out of the corrals and sweat shed. Everyone was shouting at once. Then Alvarado yelled, "Jose!" and came hurrying up. He grabbed the shearer by the hair and fairly exploded a stream of Spanish. Without another word, the shearer slunk back to his pen, grabbed a ewe, and started to shear like mad. Alvarado waved the rest of his crew back to work, and in just a minute you'd never have known anything had happened. Alvarado, who'd been going over the figures on the card with the angry tallyer, shrugged and walked away, grinning.

Somebody called for water then, and I had to run. It was getting hotter. The sun blazed down on the corrugated iron roof and the heat rose in waves that you could see. The shearers took off their shirts, and their shoulders and arms glistened with sweat. It ran off their faces in little streams.

The men would drink several dippers of water each time we were called, and some of them would take the whole bucket and pour it over their heads. We had to hustle to keep the buckets full. By mid-afternoon our faces were almost as grimy as the tromper's, and our overalls were stiff with splashed water and dust.

The shearing lasted for six days. We'd come back

to the home ranch at night so worn out we resented even the baths Mother made us take before we collapsed into bed.

One day Mother went to watch the shearing, but I don't think she liked it because she wouldn't go again. We hated to leave her alone, though she insisted she didn't mind. She said she took long walks with Molly and had discovered a beaver dam on one trip up the canyon.

"I wish she'd come with us," I told Uncle Emmet one day.

"It's no place for a woman," he said gruffly.

Mother wasn't sure it was any place for us either. She'd heard a shearer and the tallyer arguing over a count, and although it was mild compared with the argument we'd heard it still didn't set well with her. But since we were really helping Uncle Emmet, and he had no one to take our places, she couldn't very well tell us to stay away.

We learned a lot about shearing that week, just listening to the men talking at mealtime. There was a lot of argument between the shearers and wranglers about which method of shearing was best—blade or machine.

Uncle Emmet favored the blade method, of course. He argued that machines shaved the ewes too close to the skin. The blade left a good inch of wool, which protected the sheep's tender backs when exposed to the sun and also sent them into the winter with a heavier fleece to withstand the wind and snow.

On the other hand, some of the wranglers argued that it took just about half as long to shear a flock with machines and that the time saved more than made up for other disadvantages.

Of course Dan and I were on Uncle Emmet's side. By now we thought he knew everything and could never be wrong. We were proud to be related to him, and thought him, next to Dad, the finest man we'd ever known.

The last day of shearing was cloudy and quite a bit cooler. Our work slackened, so for the first time we got to watch the ewes "mother-up" with their lambs. It was something I'll never forget, and I'm sure Dan felt the same way. The ewes all looked alike to us, but not to the lambs. After they were wrangled through a gate into a corral where the ewes were waiting, each one found its mother immediately.

It was funny to watch each lamb leap stiff-legged, making a frantic dive for its own mother's teats.

"How do they *know?*" I asked Uncle Emmet.

"By the mother's bleat, maybe. Else it's just the nature of the critters."

We laughed, because that was what he always said when sheep did something nobody could understand, which was pretty often.

9. A Sheep Wagon and Bears

It seemed as if there was something new and interesting happening every day at the Rising Arrow. Right after shearing, everyone was busy getting ready to take the ewes and lambs to the National Forest Reserve for the summer.

On a twenty-thousand-acre ranch you'd think there'd be enough grazing to keep the sheep going the year round, but there was only enough, Uncle Emmet told us, for winter grazing. So all the sheepmen in that part of Montana sent their sheep high up in the mountains, where the government let them graze for a small fee.

Each sheepman had forest rights, which entitled him to a certain portion of land—allotment, Uncle Emmet called it. His allotment was located twenty-six miles straight up the mountains from the ranch, part of it at an altitude of ten thousand five hundred feet.

While Uncle Emmet was making preparations to start the sheep out he drove up to his camps every day.

Once, when he had to go to a camp which could not be reached by truck, he rode Duke and let Dan and me go along on our ponies.

We'd been riding Thunder and Lightning every afternoon since shearing, but Mother didn't want us to venture far alone, so this was a real adventure. Bastian fixed us a big lunch and we started out right after breakfast.

We rode over miles of rough country without once seeing a road or trail. But we saw a doe and her fawn drinking at a spring and a lot of pheasant and grouse. None of them seemed the least bit afraid of us. The doe just raised her head and looked at us once; then she went back to drinking again. We had gone a long way before we finally spied the sheep wagon, half hidden in a grove of quaking-aspen trees.

Uncle Emmet got off Duke, took his binoculars out of their case, and tried to locate the sheep. But it was several minutes before he spotted them in a ravine quite a distance away.

He'd brought a big roll of magazines and papers and he asked us to take them to the wagon while he rode over to talk to the herder. He told us to meet him at the same spot in about half an hour.

We'd seen sheep wagons at a distance but had never had the chance to go inside one. As we approached this one we noticed that the door was built in two sections. This seemed curious to us, but Uncle Emmet explained on the way home that the door was built that way so the herder could have plenty of air and still keep his dogs outside.

We got into the wagon by stepping on the tongue, clinging to the door handle, and hoisting ourselves inside. Inside, it was as neat as a pin, and there wasn't an inch of wasted space.

A campstove was wedged on one side, with a cupboard behind it, and on the other side a chest ran from the door to the bunk-bed. The bed was built crosswise at the far end of the wagon and had a small window above it. Opposite the long chest a shorter one stretched from the bed to the cupboard. Both chests had hinged lids that raised with rope handles. We pulled up one lid and saw that here was where the herder kept his clothes and extra supplies. Hinged to the canvas supports above the longer chest was a small table that could be drawn up out of the way when not in use.

We got so interested in looking around that we overstayed our time and found Uncle Emmet already waiting at our meeting place.

He told us on the way home that herders had to leave their wagons behind when they went on the forest. The road was too steep and rough to take them, so the herders had to sleep in tents all summer. He said tents were more convenient, anyway, because the forest rangers were strict about overgrazing the allotments and only allowed the sheep to stay on one bed-ground a short time. Then too, it was easier for Mort to move a tent over rough country.

"Of course," Uncle Emmet said, "it's not so good when bears are thick on the forest."

"Did you ever have a herder attacked by a bear?" I asked, all excited now.

He grinned. "No, but I've had a bear attacked by a herder."

He told us that bears sometimes killed sheep, but more often just plagued the herder by ripping his tent to ribbons while he was out herding his sheep. Bears love ham, bacon, or sweets of any kind, he said, and they'd claw the tents open, raid the grub boxes, and devour the food they liked best. The food they couldn't eat—such as flour, navy beans, and coffee— they'd strew on the ground.

"Why doesn't the herder lay for the bear and shoot it?"

"Because the government protects the bear, and a herder can't shoot unless he catches one in the act of killing sheep or raiding a camp."

Uncle Emmet told us about one of his herders whose camp was destroyed three times in one summer. Each time the herder reported the raid to a ranger, but the ranger wouldn't give him permission to kill the bear unless he caught it killing sheep or raiding his camp.

The herder couldn't do this. The bear had been killing sheep at night when he was asleep and raiding his camp in the daytime when he was out with his flock. So he got madder and madder. He knew Uncle Emmet would have to fire him if he broke forest regulations, but he finally got so worked up he didn't care, and one day gave Mort a note to take to the home ranch.

Uncle Emmet grinned. "He told me there was going to be one less bear on the forest next day because he wasn't going to leave the camp, or sleep, till he shot it, and he was going to do this the minute he spotted it. So he said I'd better send up a new herder. I took one up right off and we found the other herder, pleased as punch, skinning out a big black bear. Can't say I blame him much."

We were so interested in the bear stories that we could have listened the rest of the day, but we were nearing the ranch now and Uncle Emmet told us to ride on ahead and tell Mother we were safe while he stopped in the field to check up on an irrigation ditch with Shorty.

10. Nicky, the Famous Lead Sheep

Two days later the four bands of sheep started into the mountains. Dan and I were wild to go on the drive, but Uncle Emmet said he might be gone several days and he'd rather not take us. When he saw how disappointed we were he told us we could ride our ponies along as far as the counting corrals, eight miles from the ranch. This was where the rangers counted the sheep into the forest.

It was on this trip that we first saw Nicky, the bell-wether. We'd learned that each band had a bell, or lead sheep. Sometimes it would be a wise old ewe, sometimes a wether that had been a "bum," or orphan lamb, raised at the ranch on a bottle. Nicky had been a "bum." Bastian raised him and was still fond of him and very proud of him. Bastian had told us a lot of stories about Nicky, and one of them was especially interesting.

A bell sheep, Bastian said, had to be adventurous and willing to go over narrow bridges—which most sheep fear—over dangerous mountain trails, and streams of swift water. But even the lead sheep had to be persuaded, so the herder usually took a slice of bread and doled it out bit by bit until the hazardous crossing had been made. The minute the lead sheep started out, the rest of the band would follow blindly.

But Nicky wouldn't go into action for a piece of bread. He had to be lured with a cigarette. (His name was really Nicotine and had been shortened to Nicky.) Nicky had developed the bad habit of eating cigarettes when he was a half-grown lamb. Most of the ranch men rolled their own cigarettes, but Bastian smoked tailor-mades, and one day when he was taking garbage out to the pit he lost a full pack from his pocket. He went back to look for it and surprised Nicky calmly eating it, paper and all.

The ranch hands thought this was funny when Bastian told them about it, and they often fed the lamb cigarettes just to watch his foolish antics. Finally Nicky got to be a nuisance. Every time he caught sight of one of the men smoking a cigarette he'd rush him and try frantically to get it.

Nicky grew into a very big sheep, and a strong one too. The men didn't think it was so funny any longer when Nicky started butting and lunging at them, and when he knocked one of them flat and laid him up for a week with a bad back Uncle Emmet decided he'd have to do something about it. So he sent Nicky up to the flock of a Mormon herder who didn't smoke at all.

Nicky hadn't been in the herd two weeks before the herder began to complain every time Mort showed up with supplies. He said Nicky wouldn't lead unless the notion struck him, and when it did he'd usually light out with half the herd at his heels. The dogs had to round up the ewes so often they were getting footsore, and besides, so much "dogging" wasn't good for his sheep.

The herder demanded a new lead sheep. There was none on hand at the time. It was mid-winter, and the snow was so deep that Mort had to take supplies to the Mormon's camp on a pack horse. He told the man to tie Nicky up until he could get a buckboard through the drifts and haul him back to the home ranch.

Bastian said that was one of the worst winters he'd ever seen in Montana. The snow got deeper and deeper, and Mort packed supplies on Dolly and Blue until early spring. Every time he went to the Mormon's camp he'd see Nicky tied to the wagon wheel, but he had too many other things to worry about to give him a thought.

One day in early spring the herder sent word by a ranger that four hundred of his ewes were trapped on an ice gorge and he couldn't get to them. Even the dogs couldn't get close enough to budge them. Every man on the ranch, including Bastian, went right down to the river to see what could be done.

The sheep were huddled together on a pile of upturned ice, with a big sheet of level ice between them and the shore. If there'd been time, Bastian said, the men might have been able to pack the ewes down one by one, but the gorge was already beginning to shift. At any minute it might break. Then its force would crack the surrounding ice and the sheep would have a pile-up in the river and drown.

Uncle Emmet had just decided to take his loss and go home, when Bastian let out a whoop and called to the herder, "Ain't that Nicky up in front?"

The herder got red in the face and admitted that Nicky had slipped his halter several days before and that he hadn't got around to cutting him out from the herd and tying him up again.

Bastian stepped onto the ice, got down on his hands and knees, and crawled as close as he could to the gorge. Then he shouted, "Nicky!" Nicky was calmly chewing his cud and he eyed Bastian as if he didn't even know him. But when Bastian pulled out a pack of cigarettes, Nicky's head came up with a jerk, and he leaped up as if he'd been shot from a gun. The rest of the herd leaped too. They followed Nicky across that ice on the run.

"If I'd been a split second slower I'd never have made it to shore," Bastian said. "There'd have been a pile-up, and I'd have been on the bottom."

After that story we were eager to see Nicky of course.

The day we rode up to the counting corrals Nicky was leading the band we followed. The sheep were two-year-old ewes and hard to handle. They balked several times on bridges, and each time this happened, the herder would take a package of cigarettes out of his pocket, give one to Nicky and walk ahead quickly, holding the pack up in his hand. When the crossing was made he'd reward Nicky with another cigarette; then he would hide his package away for the next emergency.

Nicky was the biggest sheep I ever saw. He seemed different from the rest because he held his head high and walked with a sort of strut. He was the most famous lead sheep in that part of the country, Uncle Emmet told us. He'd even go through a brush fire if he knew he'd get a cigarette when he reached the other side. And because he could be depended upon to lead under any circumstance, other sheepmen often borrowed him when they had to take their herds over extra-rough crossings.

Dan said, "I wish we were going to be here during lambing so we could raise a bellwether."

Uncle Emmet pushed his hat back and smiled. "Derned if I don't wish you could be too."

Of course we knew that we couldn't, so we never even hoped.

11. Virginia City and the Vigilantes

Before haying started Uncle Emmet took Mother and Dan and me over to Virginia City for the day. The mountain didn't seem nearly as steep as it had the first time we drove over it. We were getting used to high mountains, I guess.

On our way into town we passed the gray stone museum that Mort had pointed out to us before. Uncle Emmet told us that a man named Thompson had built the museum, which was also a library, and had given it to Virginia City because he'd made his fortune there in the gold mines and was grateful. We wanted to stop, but Uncle Emmet said we'd enjoy it more after we'd seen the rest of the town.

We began sight-seeing at the far end of the street and went first into an old theater. Nobody was around at that time of the morning, but Uncle Emmet said they had a very good company, which put on very old plays and variety shows several nights a week. There was nothing much to see at the theater, so we walked on up the street.

We passed an old-time saloon called The Bale of Hay. We didn't go in, but Uncle Emmet told us it was just like the saloon where Clubfoot George and the rest of the road agents had hung out in the gold-rush days. We did see the barkeeper. He came out while we were standing on the sidewalk, and he looked just like the barkeepers we'd seen in Western movies, with a handle-bar mustache and an apron tied around his waist.

We crossed the street and looked into the window of a little dressmaking shop that fascinated Mother. The window was full of things such as pointed high-button shoes, corsets, silly little umbrellas, lace muffs, and blouses with enormous balloon sleeves. Inside, the wax figure of a lady—in a dress with a very full skirt and tight waist—sat at a funny little sewing machine. Other wax figures, supposed to be lady customers, were standing around dressed the same way. Mother loved it and stayed on long after the rest of us were ready to leave. She said it made her feel just as if she had lived back in the sixties.

We finally persuaded her to leave. Then we went to the newspaper office and saw the old printing press and a few copies of the first Virginia City newspapers. The Fairweather Inn was close, so we went there next. It must have been very grand in earlier days.

The parlor downstairs had a lot of plush and gilt furniture in it, and fancy lamps and carpets. The bedrooms were furnished with big mahogany beds and flowered carpets and bureaus with marble tops.

Dan and I weren't as interested in the Fairweather Inn as we were in the Wells-Fargo express office across the street. There were wax figures there too—a mustached man weighing up gold dust on some scales, a full-skirted lady getting ready to take the stagecoach, and another man, standing beside some queer old trunks and valises.

But the thing we liked best was a big barn where the honest citizens of Virginia City had gathered in 1864 to form a vigilante committee. Uncle Emmet told us about the vigilantes, and it was an exciting story. He said that many of the men who came to Virginia City in the beginning were army deserters and criminals wanted by the law in other states. They banded together and decided there were easier ways to get gold than to dig it out of the ground. So they held up shipment after shipment of gold and wouldn't stop at anything, even murder, to get it.

Nobody knew who they were because they wore masks, and even masked their horses by throwing blankets over them. Nobody was safe from them, so the decent people banded together and swore they'd hunt down every one of the road agents and hang them. It took quite a while, but the vigilantes finally cleaned up the town. We saw the one-story building up the street where the hangings had taken place. It made me feel kind of creepy to see the scaffold and imagine the road agents dangling there.

Next Uncle Emmet drove us up the steep grade to Boot Hill and we saw the road agents' graves. While we were there Uncle Emmet pointed out another hill, which he called Bummer Dan's Bar. He said one of the earliest settlers had been a bum named Dan McFadden. He bummed his meals, his drinks, his tobacco, and even a place to sleep. The miners were good-natured about it, but when he began to bum gold dust so he could gamble they got mad and told him to get to work or get out. They told him to locate a claim and dig his own gold.

Dan said he didn't know where to dig. They said one place was as good as another, and one of them, for a joke, pointed to a bleak hillside that looked so unpromising no one had bothered to stake out a claim. So Dan bummed a pick, a shovel, a bucket, and some rope. Then he sank a shaft on the bare hill. The joke was on the other miners, because that shaft produced over five million dollars in gold! After that the hill was always called Bummer Dan's Bar.

After lunch we went back to the museum, and it was so interesting we spent a couple of hours there. It was crammed with old, curious things. There were oxen yokes, ore specimens, old books, pictures and records, and old grocery bills showing the high prices the settlers had to pay for their food. I remember that one of them listed flour at one hundred dollars for a hundred pounds!

We saw a lot of freakish things too—a petrified cat, a lamb with one head and two bodies, and a walking fish called an axolotl. It looked like a fish, but it had four legs. Uncle Emmet said there were a lot of them in Axolotl Lake, which was only seven miles from the ranch; and he said the fish often walked that far. We also saw Clubfoot George's foot, and it looked just as Mort had said it did. Uncle Emmet really laughed when Mother tried to steer us away from it before we got a good look.

After we left the museum Uncle Emmet drove us up Alder Gulch to see a monument that marked the place where gold was first discovered. Then he drove several miles farther so that Dan and I could look for rubies and garnets in the gravel mounds. Dan found a small ruby. Uncle Emmet said it was flawed and could never be properly cut. But Dan was proud of it, anyway, and we both hoped we could come back someday and maybe find a ruby as big as Mort's.

We got to the ranch just before supper. We'd had a wonderful time, but not nearly as wonderful as we had every day at the Rising Arrow.

12. News of Dad

The next morning as we started out for the field with our pails of poisoned oats, Uncle Emmet stopped us. "Let the gophers go for a while," he said. "We start haying tomorrow. Can't take a chance on the work horses' getting poisoned."

We were sorry, because we were both fair marksmen by now and had been taking the rifle to the field for some time. Of course this wasn't really satisfactory, because if one of us spotted a stray gopher the other was sure to be carrying the gun. But the very fact that we'd earned the right to carry the rifle meant a lot to us. We felt as if we were losing a friend when we put the rifle away that morning.

"I don't see why we can't hunt gophers somewhere else," Dan complained. "They're all over the place."

I agreed with him, and asked Uncle Emmet if we couldn't hunt up in the canyon near the garden. "There are lots of gophers there."

"No," he said kind of shortly. "You let that rifle alone."

I felt as if I'd been slapped in the face. Dan and I had put out several hundred pounds of poisoned oats and killed nearly fifty gophers, and it seemed as if Uncle Emmet might have been halfway civil, or at least have told us we'd done pretty well.

But Uncle Emmet had a better way of telling us. He went into his office and came out with two shiny new Remington .22-caliber rifles.

"Use your own guns after this," he said, handing them to us. "And don't forget what I told you about walking abreast when you're hunting and always pointing the muzzle of the gun toward the ground until you're ready to aim."

He cautioned us some more, but we were so excited

about owning rifles of our own that neither of us could remember afterward what he had said.

For the next two weeks we hunted on foot or rode Lightning and Thunder to explore every inch of the canyon. We got so brown that Mother said we looked like a couple of Indians. We were surprised because Mother never objected any more to our riding, or even hunting, as long as we left the guns at home when we rode horseback. She seemed to have got over all her fears for us.

But in other ways Mother wasn't like herself. As the summer drew to a close she got thinner, and she never wanted to go any place with us any more. When the telephone rang she'd jump to answer it, and on Wednesdays and Saturdays when Mort went to Virginia City for the mail she was restless until the time for him to come home. Then she'd stand at the window, watching for the truck. After the mail was sorted she'd go to her room and stay there until supper.

One afternoon we persuaded her to ride down to the field to watch the men hay, but she wouldn't stay but a few minutes after we got there. I rode back with her to unsaddle Dolly, and later I fussed about it to Bastian. "Mother never wants to do anything that's fun any more."

Mort said scoldingly, "You be patient with her.

She don't want to leave that telephone. She thinks she might hear about your pa."

Later, Bastian—who is superstitious and believes in omens—said Mother must have sensed something.

Anyway, I was sorry I'd been cross that day, and I ran up the stairs and told Mother so. She hugged me and said, "Were you cross, darling? I hadn't noticed."

And then I knew she'd been worrying about Dad all along and had just been pretending that she wasn't upset so we'd have a happy summer.

Dan and I missed Dad all the time, but since we'd come to the Rising Arrow and talked to Uncle Emmet about it we never doubted that he'd come back someday.

Of course there were times when we missed him more than others—like the day we'd spent in Virginia City and I thought that if Dad were along he'd write an article about it. I could just see him making notes in his little brown book. I wanted to cry. Sometimes— it's queer—Dan and I each know what the other is thinking, and that time Dan said in a choky voice, "I wish Dad were here."

And Uncle Emmet was cheerful. "Next summer you'll have to persuade your Dad to come up and do an article about the restoration of Virginia City," he had said.

Then I felt better and *knew* we'd get some news soon. But I didn't dream how soon.

One day a hay man had a sunstroke, and that left the crew shorthanded. Uncle Emmet came back to the house and took Dan and me down to clean up the loose hay around the stack. It was backbreaking work, and at quitting time we were so tired it was all we could do to hoist ourselves into the back of the truck.

We were trudging along toward the house from the barn and thinking we'd never make it when Mother burst through the gate, calling our names and running toward us. "Dad's alive!" She caught us to her and kept saying over and over, "Dad's alive!"

She was laughing and crying at the same time, but her eyes were big and alive and happy. When we reached the house she calmed down and told us that Dad had been wounded in the leg by a Red sniper, and a South Korean family had taken him in and hidden him from the North Korean troops. Dad had almost died of pneumonia and infection before the United Nations troops recaptured the village.

"The leg is still bad," Mother told us. "The first of September they're flying him to a base hospital in San Francisco for an operation."

That was just ten days away. We were so happy about Dad that we forgot we'd been tired. The three of us sat down together and planned—we'd rent our house in Springfield for the winter and get an apartment in San Francisco, where Dan and I would go to school.

"The only thing that worries me," Mother told Uncle Emmet when he got home, "is that it will leave the boys pretty much alone. I'll want to be with Paul every minute I can."

"You're leaving the boys right here," Uncle Emmet announced firmly.

Mother looked relieved for a minute; then she became very serious and said, "What about school?"

"There's a country school just three miles from here."

"Three miles! How will they get there when the weather turns bad?"

"Ride horseback, like the rest of the kids."

Mother shook her head. "No. They might get lost in a blizzard."

And she wouldn't agree to our staying until Uncle Emmet gave her his word that he'd take us to school in case of a blizzard.

For the next ten days she thought of dozens of other things to worry about. Suppose we got sick, broke bones, stumbled into an old prospect hole! Uncle Emmet was very patient with her for someone who didn't care for women. As fast as she'd think up a new worry he'd talk her out of it, but each time we were afraid he couldn't, and that she'd change her mind and tell him we couldn't stay.

13. Mother Goes to San Francisco

Mother left for San Francisco late in August. We went to Dillon with Uncle Emmet to see her off on the train. She hated to leave us—I could tell how much by the way she tried to keep us from knowing. She was very gay and talked a lot about what a celebration we'd have when Dad got well enough to travel home. But we were trying, too, to keep her from seeing how bad we felt. I don't think we realized until that day how much we were going to miss her. I had to swallow hard to keep from crying, and Dan had tears in his eyes when the train began to pull away from the station.

"Bad luck to watch a train go!" Uncle Emmet said gruffly, and then his voice got gentle and he said, "Let's go over to the Andrus Hotel and put a steak under our belts before we start home."

He always knew what to do. The steaks and a huge platter of french-fried potatoes did make us feel better, and all the time we were eating, Uncle Emmet talked about things we'd do on the ranch that winter. When we finished dinner he said, "Might as well buy your winter clothes while we're here." He paid the check and led us around the corner to a men's clothing store.

It took all three of us to carry the things he bought to the car. There were boots and overshoes, woolen underwear, shirts and socks, sheep-lined coats and fancy chaps, fur caps and fur-lined mittens. And we didn't get them any too soon. It turned cold the very next week.

School didn't start until the end of September, and this was a break for Dan and me because it gave us the chance to go on the lamb drive.

In the meantime we missed Mother terribly. I think even Uncle Emmet and Bastian missed her a little. But Molly missed her the most. The night we got home from taking Mother to the train Molly rushed up to greet us, and when she didn't see Mother she began to whine and run around the room as though she were looking for her. After a minute she sat down on her haunches in front of Uncle Emmet and barked, just once but very loud, as if she were asking a question.

Uncle Emmet understands dogs the way he understands people. He put his hand on her head and said, "Helen's gone, Molly, but never fear, she'll be back one of these days."

I know Molly understood, because she stopped hunting for Mother and went over and lay down in her corner with her head on her paws. All the next day she grieved, though, and didn't seem interested in anything.

"Never seen her take to anybody the way she took to your ma," Bastian said. "She's a great old dog and don't you ever forget it. Remind me someday when I'm not busy to tell you how she outfoxed a blizzard and saved a whole band of sheep."

This was the second time someone had promised to tell us the story, and of course we begged Bastian to tell it right away. But Bastian was going to cook on the lamb drive and he was in the cellar checking over the supplies he would need.

"I can't spin yarns and keep my mind on this list," he said. "When the lamb drive's over you remind me and I'll tell you a tale that'll make your hair stand on end."

14. Nicky at Work

The sheep were still in the mountains, and Uncle Emmet had ordered his railroad cars and expected to ship the lambs to Chicago on the tenth of September. We started up to the forest on the fifth, driving with Uncle Emmet in the pick-up. Mort and Bastian followed in the big truck, which would serve as the chuck wagon on the drive.

Snow lay all over the mountains that morning, but it was not deep enough to stop the shipping. We left the ranch before daybreak and arrived at the headquarters camp on Uncle Emmet's allotment around ten o'clock.

All four bands of sheep were there waiting, but the ewes would not be brought out of the forest until after the lambs were shipped. The lambs had doubled in size since we saw them last. They were almost as big as their mothers, and they made more noise. It was all very exciting—the sheep bleated furiously, the dogs raced and barked, the men waved sacks and "tin dogs" (cans strung on wires, which made an awful racket) and shouted at the top of their lungs.

Dan and I sat on the corral fence to watch the cutting. The wind was raw, and we turned up the collars of our sheep-skin coats and were grateful that Uncle Emmet had bought them for us.

When the last band was cut we saw Nicky again. Bastian told us proudly that Nicky would lead the drive. But Nicky wasn't pleased about it. He rolled his eyes and hung back when they turned him into the corral with the lambs, and bleated pitifully. We soon saw why he objected. The lambs, missing their mothers, rushed him, nuzzled him, sucked on any part of him they could reach, from his ears to his hoofs. He tried to fight them off, butting and backing, but he couldn't escape. There were over five thousand lambs, and they were too many for even a bold bell-wether like Nicky.

At four o'clock the lambs, with Nicky and a herder at their head, started down the mountains. Bastian and Mort and Uncle Emmet went ahead in the trucks to Clover Meadows, where they'd make camp for the night. Dan and I walked with the wranglers.

The lambs were frantic because their mothers were left behind. They kept trying to turn back, and the dogs had a hard time holding them. We all raced back and forth, waving and shouting, but on a mountain called Lazy Man's Hill several hundred got away from us and one of the wranglers took a dog and went back to look for them. He found them and brought them into camp long after dark.

The rest of us reached the first night's camp at dusk. Bastian and Mort had set up the tepees and tents and had supper ready. I don't think any meal I ever ate tasted quite so good as that one, although we had only fried ham, bread, and canned pork and beans.

That night we slept in sleeping bags in a tepee. It seemed as if we'd just closed our eyes when Uncle Emmet shook us and told us breakfast was ready. It was still dark when we stumbled over to the creek to wash our faces in the stinging cold water. There was no wind that morning, but the air smelled wonderful.

The fragrance of the bacon Bastian was frying on a campfire mingled with the scent of fir and pine and spruce and made us so hungry we raced each other back to camp.

We started out again at dawn. Uncle Emmet, having got the lambs under way, went off in his truck to make some arrangements at the shipping point. Dan and I followed the lambs with the men. The first few miles we thought it was going to storm. Clouds boiled over the mountains and settled in the hollows. We followed the high ridges and walked through clouds for several hours. Then the sun came out, and the snow sparkled as though it had diamonds on it.

The lambs stayed together that day and the dogs didn't have so much racing to do. But Mort warned us that the real job would begin when we reached the highway and began to meet passing cars. We discovered how right he was, for the next day we made only half as many miles, and those miles were awful.

Passing cars frightened the lambs, and the ones in the rear, cut off from the ones in front that Nicky was leading, would try to turn back or refuse to go at all. Mort had given both Dan and me "tin dogs," and we raced back and forth, making an awful clatter and startling the balky lambs into motion. The sheep dogs barked and nipped at the lambs' shanks, trying to turn them, but most of the time Nicky had to be led to the rear to get them moving again. This happened a dozen times before we made camp that night, and Dan and I were so tired and sleepy it was all we could do to hold out until supper was over.

The next day was worse, because the highway climbed into the mountains again. In some places the road was so narrow and steep that it gave me a queer, dizzy feeling when I looked down into the gorges. That night we made camp on top of the mountain. Below we could see the twinkling lights of Norris, the shipping point. I think everyone was relieved at this sight—even the dogs.

The loading was to start at eight o'clock next morning. When we reached the stockyards corrals there were a number of double-decked truckloads of lambs there ahead of us. We helped corral the Rising Arrow lambs and then sat on the fence and watched the trucks of the other shippers unload into another corral.

"I'd think it would be easier to truck the Rising Arrow lambs," I said to Uncle Emmet.

"It would be if we were closer to the railroad," he said. "I've tried it both ways and found the lambs don't shrink as much on a long drive if they can graze some on the way."

Norris was just thirty miles from the ranch, and Dan asked Uncle Emmet why he hadn't met us there.

Uncle Emmet said that the railroad was used only to ship stock in the fall and to freight in supplies the rest of the year.

"Why don't they have passenger cars?" I asked.

Uncle Emmet chuckled. "The last passenger train that came in here got snowed clear under. They sent in a rotary snow plow to dig it out and the plow got snowed under. The train and plow stayed there until spring. I guess that sort of discouraged the railroad people."

Just then the engine puffed up the track, stopping the first double-decked car in front of a loading chute. Now we saw Nicky in action. Head in air, he stalked into the narrow chute, ran swiftly up the ramp, and paused in the car door. The lambs raced after him, pressing him close. When the chute was full, Nicky ambled slowly into the car and moved to the far end, where he stayed until the car had its full number of lambs. Then Uncle Emmet whistled and shouted, "Nicky!" Nicky sneaked along the side of the car and escaped from the door before the lambs, jammed closely together, could follow.

It was the funniest thing to see Nicky leap out. He looked so happy and smug. It was just as if he were thinking: Well, there's one bunch that won't plague me any more. He duped the Rising Arrow lambs over and over, and if ever a bellwether enjoyed a job that wether was Nicky.

15. Molly the Sheep Dog

There wasn't much work done on the Rising Arrow the day after the lambs were shipped. Everyone was worn out from the drive, even Uncle Emmet. But the next day the men had to move the sheep wagons back up on the range so they'd be ready when the herders brought their bands off the forest.

Uncle Emmet gave us the job of oiling harnesses in the barn that morning. When we came in at noon, old Molly greeted us noisily; then she went over and lay down in her corner. I think she still missed Mother and was more friendly with us because we belonged to Mother.

We petted her for a while, and that made me remember the story Bastian had promised to tell us. After dinner we offered to wash dishes while Bastian got his bread in the oven and fried the doughnuts for supper.

"You can talk while you work," I said. "Why don't you tell us that story about Molly?"

Bastian flipped a half-dozen doughnuts into an iron

skillet half full of sizzling grease and speared and turned them around with a fork. Then he said, "Might as well."

For the next half-hour we listened to one of the strangest stories we'd ever heard.

Bastian said Molly almost hadn't been a working sheep dog. She'd been the runt of a litter, and Uncle Emmet never would have taken her to a sheep camp to be trained if he hadn't been short of dogs at the time.

Molly got off to a bad start because Mac, the herder, had expected a huskier dog, and a male in the bargain. At first he didn't like Molly and was impatient with her. Bastian said most sheep dogs are devoted to their masters and care very little for the sheep. But it was different with Molly. When Mac scolded her and showed that he liked the older dog better, she gave all her love to the sheep.

There are two dogs in each of the Rising Arrow herds, Bastian said. There's an older dog who knows all the herder's signals and a younger dog who gets to know the signals by watching the other dog work and imitating him.

Bastian said a herder had to signal because he's often too far from the dogs to make his voice heard. So he stands back where the dogs can see him and signals. If he gestures to the right or the left the sheep are supposed to be turned in that direction. If he raises both arms above his head the dogs know he wants them to hold the sheep where they are.

But from the first Molly knew more about the habits of the sheep than of the herder. For one thing, she always knew when a "marker" was missing.

"What's a 'marker'?" Dan asked.

"A black sheep," Bastian answered. "There's one black sheep for every hundred white sheep in the herd, so when a marker's missing the herder knows white sheep're missing too, because sheep never stray off alone."

He said the herder had to climb to some point above the herd to count the black sheep. Molly didn't. She just knew when some were gone. Several times the herder saw her race away suddenly, disappear, and come back after a while with a bunch of strays, and always a marker was among them. This saved Mac a lot of trouble and pleased him so much that he grew fond of Molly and came to depend on her to keep track of the sheep. But Molly didn't forget that he hadn't always felt this way. She never grew fond of Mac.

As Molly grew older and learned all the signals she often ignored them, and the herder began to notice that when she did disobey, it always turned out that she was right—such as the time he signaled for the sheep to be turned into a quaking-aspen grove to the right. Molly deliberately turned them the other way, and snapped and snarled so hard at the other dog for interfering that it finally got in and helped her.

Mac was furious because the two dogs were moving the sheep as fast as they could in the other direction. He could see it was Molly's fault, so he cut a stick and set out on a run, meaning to punish her as soon as he could catch her. He had gone only a little way when he saw a big cinnamon bear come loping out of the quaking-aspen grove, making straight for the herd. But by now Molly was holding the sheep quite a distance away, and the herder was able to shoot the bear before it did any damage.

Whenever Mac came to the ranch he used to brag about the way Molly worked. Bastian said herders always brag about their dogs, and sometimes even fib, so when Mac told the bear story nobody believed him. Then Molly proved him so right that he could have told the tallest kind of yarn and everyone at the ranch would have taken it for fact.

One afternoon when Mac was grazing his sheep quite a way from his wagon a sudden blizzard came up. The weather had been threatening all morning, and he'd already started the herd back toward the wagon, but now he dogged them as fast as he could.

The worst of the storm caught them a mile from the wagon. The herder couldn't see the sheep for the whirling snow; he couldn't even see his hand before him. But he knew the general direction of his wagon and pushed on as fast as he could. In his haste he was careless; he forgot an old prospect hole, stumbled into it, and broke his leg.

He had a terrible time hoisting himself out of the hole, but finally made it and crawled the rest of the way to the wagon, thinking the dogs had taken the sheep on ahead. But the sheep were nowhere in sight when he reached camp. Mac was half crazy from pain and exposure. He worried about the fate of his flock, but there was nothing he could do but wait until the next day, when he expected Mort to bring some supplies.

The blizzard turned out to be one of the worst they'd ever had in Montana, so Mort didn't get to Mac's camp until the next night. And then he never would have made it if he hadn't come on horseback. The older dog came back to camp that same night, and Mort and Mac decided that the sheep had scattered and Molly was dead.

"She'd be back if she wasn't," Mac said.

It stopped storming around noon of next day. Mac's leg was paining him terribly, and Mort decided he'd have to try to get him back to the ranch. Mort walked and put Mac on the horse. The snow was piled in great drifts that reached to the horse's belly. They pushed on as fast as they could, but three hours later they'd only made as many miles.

They were passing a ridge of huge, upturned rocks

when they heard a wild barking. A moment later Molly came bounding through the snow toward them. Mort searched the countryside with his binoculars and could see no sheep. They called Molly and started on.

But Molly refused to go. She raced back and forth, barking and whining. Mort lost his patience and wanted to leave her. But the herder, in spite of his pain, refused to go. He said Molly never did anything without a reason and insisted that Mort go with her and investigate.

The minute Mort started back Molly dodged around the edge of the cliff and down into the gulch. Mort followed, and could hardly believe what he saw. Molly had the entire herd bedded down in a little clearing beneath the rocks that never could have been seen from the trail! The sheep were safe; but for Molly they would all have scattered and died.

"So that's why the boss thinks so much of Molly," Bastian said in conclusion. "And that's why every sheep dog on this place comes from one of her litters."

16. School in the Mountains

The haying had been delayed by the lamb drive and the last crop of alfalfa still lay in windrows. Uncle Emmet told us that from now on it would be a race with time to get the hay in stacks before winter set in. Already the aspen, willow, and cottonwood that grew along Wigwam Creek had turned to yellow and gold, and most of the birds that nested there were on their way south. The men worked long hours to get the crop in.

We started to school at the end of September. We weren't happy about it. There were so many interesting things to do at the ranch. Mort had to fix a fence in the neighborhood of the schoolhouse that morning, and we rode part of the way with him.

"What's the teacher like?" Dan asked as we rode along.

"Mrs. Morton's a fine little lady," Mort said. "Widder of a dry rancher."

A dry rancher, he explained, was someone who had homesteaded years before, when the government gave land to people for living on it three years and fencing it in and building a cabin. He told us some interesting stories about city people who had come to Montana and taken up homesteads without knowing a thing about ranching or farming or water rights.

"They'd maybe pick out a homestead because there was a nice little creek running over one corner of it, and then they'd find they couldn't use an inch of the water for irrigating."

"But why not? The creek was on their land."

"Because the district court had allotted the water years before to ranchers downstream from them." Mort said the ownership of the water from all the streams in Montana was decreed by law, and it was illegal for anyone but the owners to use it. Most of the land open to homesteaders at that time had no water rights. He said you couldn't make a go of a farm or ranch in Montana unless you had water rights.

"City people'd come out maybe after a wet season and the range'd be green and flourishin'. Thinkin' they'd struck pay dirt, they'd sink all their money into improvements. Then a drought'd come and they wouldn't have enough grass to graze a flea. So they'd have to starve or go back where they come from. Most of them went back. I could show you a dozen deserted homesteads within twenty miles of the ranch."

"Why did Mrs. Morton stay?"

"Because she's one of the few that's got a little water on her place." Mort pulled up his horse on the brow of a hill and pointed. "There's your school, boys. I'll be leavin' you here."

We'd seen the school several times from a distance, but that was before we'd had any idea we'd be attending it. Now we eyed it curiously.

It was a small log building, not even as big as the Rising Arrow bunkhouse. But it was big enough, we soon discovered. There were only six other pupils beside Dan and me, four girls and two boys. Two of the girls were in classes with us; the rest of the children were younger.

Mrs. Morton was a plump little white-haired lady, much older than we'd expected. She looked easygoing and friendly. She turned out to be friendly as long as we behaved, but she wasn't easygoing. She was the strictest teacher we'd ever had. If we failed to prepare our lessons she kept us in after school until we knew them perfectly. Dan and I begrudged every minute we had to spend away from the Rising Arrow so we didn't get kept in after school many times.

We got a letter from Mother a week after she reached San Francisco. It was full of news about Dad, and such a happy letter that we both felt happy too. She wrote:

> I guess I'm good medicine for Dad, because he wanted to know when he could sit up this morning, and the nurse said he hadn't cared before.

She said the doctors had told her that Dad would be in the hospital until spring, if not longer, because they had to graft bone in his leg and that would mean two operations.

We wrote letters to Mother and Dad every Sunday, telling them what we'd done the past week. There was a lot to tell, because in late October, Uncle Emmet began to make preparations for the winter. He explained that he had to get his hauling done early, before the roads were snowed in.

For a week the trucks were on the road every day, hauling groceries, salt and corn, coal for heating, gasoline and oil, and spare parts for the ranch trucks and tractors.

Now that haying was over, the crew dwindled to

Bastian, Mort, Bill, and Shorty—the regulars—who would stay all winter. Shorty and Bill dug potatoes, onions, carrots, and rutabagas; pulled cabbage, squash, and pumpkins. One Saturday they let Dan and me drive the wagons heaped with vegetables from the garden to the root-cellar. When they'd all been stored in their bins we sorted the cabbages and Bastian shredded the smaller, imperfect heads and tamped them down in kegs with layers of salt, to make sauerkraut.

After that all hands turned in for hog-killing. Uncle Emmet shot the hogs between the eyes with his Luger. Each hog had hardly stopped kicking before it was doused in a vat of scalding water, then hoisted and swung by its hind legs from a scaffold. Mort scraped the bristles off right down to the smooth white skin; then he flopped the carcass onto a long table, where Bastian and Shorty took over and sawed and sliced until they had tub after tub full of hams, shoulders, bacon, ribs, backbone, and solid chunks of pork chops. When they had finished this job the meat was separated and the meat to be cured taken to the smokehouse.

Next the lard was rendered out in big black kettles over a leaping birch fire. The lard had to be stirred often to keep it from burning, and Dan and I took turns stirring with wooden ax handles.

We helped to make the sausage too, and our fingers

got stiff with cold as we cut sausage meat into chunks that would go through the grinder. After the meat was all ground (and there were several tubfuls), we helped mix in the sage and salt and pepper for seasoning before it was stuffed into empty salt sacks and dipped in paraffin.

At the end of two weeks the cellar and the smokehouse were full and all the hauling had been done. Everyone was pleased to be finished, and Uncle Emmet said, "Now let it storm. We're fixed up for the winter." That night all the men went to town to celebrate; and Uncle Emmet said he guessed we'd better celebrate too, so he took us to town for supper and a picture show—the first we'd seen since we left Springfield.

17. Sassy the Beaver

There was a heavy snow in early November. It wasn't like any snow we'd seen before. It lay on the ground and piled higher every day. Then the wind began to blow, and great drifts banked against the house, barn, sheds, and fences.

The wind was so high one Saturday morning that Uncle Emmet warned us not to ride our horses. "It's foolishness!" He scoffed. "You could look out for yourselves. But I promised your mother I wouldn't let you take any chances. You know how women are."

We hung around the house until after dinner and then got on our coats and overshoes and went out to the barn, where we found Mort sitting on the floor, sorting and mending traps. He told us he'd trapped quite a few mink and muskrat and coyote the past few winters. He used to set his traps on the way to the camps and check them on his way back.

"I could trap twice as many if I had time to set traps and check on them."

"Could we learn to trap?" I asked.

"Sure," Mort answered. "Trappin's easy, if you got the knowhow. And you'd have plenty of time to look them over on your way home from school." He explained that you should check every trap you set every day.

"Do you catch something every day?" Dan asked, excited.

" 'Tain't that so much as you *might* trap somethin', and you couldn't leave a poor dumb critter to suffer. Then too, I've had some critters chew a foot clear off and get loose. Beaver's the worst to do that. I quit usin' steel traps on them and took to puttin' box traps under water. I figgered drownin' was easier than bleedin' to death."

We could see Mort was in a story-telling mood, so we offered to help him mend traps, and while we worked he told us a lot about beavers. He said they were the hardest animals to trap; that they were smarter than human beings. He told us they got so thick up the canyon one year that they dammed up the creek until not a trickle of water got to the garden.

"You can't trap one of the critters in Montana unless you can prove they're damagin' property or cuttin' off the water supply," Mort said. "So the boss got the game warden out to look the dams over. He agreed right off to the trappin', but it was the spring of the year, when beaver's fur ain't prime, so he told us to trap them alive and he'd haul them upcountry. And I got the trappin' job."

Mort said he trapped around fifteen beavers in box traps; then the warden came in his truck and hauled them away. But one big mother beaver was too smart for Mort. Every time he set a trap under water she'd find a way to spring it and go right on damming up the creek.

"I was so mad I could've killed her with my bare hands." Mort chuckled. "She outfoxed me all summer, but she finally got hers in the fall. I figgered she must've slipped and sprung the trap accidentally."

"Did the game warden haul her up with the others?" I asked.

Mort looked kind of foolish; then he laughed. "No. That was four years ago, and she's still buildin' dams in the same place."

"But you said you trapped her."

"Oh, I got her all right, but it was this way: one morning when I went up to look at the trap I heard somethin' that sounded like children cryin'. When I got to the pond I seen two beaver kittens swimmin' in circles just above the last trap I'd set. And they *was* cryin' too, so pitiful it made me feel mean and ornery. So I set out to look for their old lady, and there she was, caught hard and fast. She hadn't been there long because she was still kickin'.

"I got her out double fast and was fixin' to put her out of her misery when them kittens began squallin' again. Know what I done? I hauled her up on the bank, worked the water out of her lungs. Derned if I didn't even breathe in her mouth to bring her to. She came to life snarlin' and fightin', and I had to tie her up. Then I began to look for her kittens, but they'd hid out in the brush and I couldn't find a trace of them. I couldn't leave 'em to starve, so I just turned the old girl loose.

"Now don't you tell the boss what I done," he warned, grinning.

"Boss figgered the old girl was too smart to be trapped. I got kind of attached to her, and now I just sneak up and tear out her dams when she gets too busy. But it's gettin' hard work now that several litters of her kittens is grown and can help her."

Mort said he'd got to know her so well in four years that he'd even given her a name. He called her Sassy!

That night Dan asked Uncle Emmet if we could try our hands at trapping, and he seemed real pleased. He said there were lots of traps in the blacksmith shop and we could use as many as we wanted. Mort promised to show us how to set them the first day he was free.

18. A Montana Blizzard

It began to get bitter cold early in December. Dan and I had thought it was cold before, but we discovered that the fall weather had been mild according to Montana standards. Most of the time we'd been able to cut across the hills to school, but on several days, when the wind was high and the snow drifting, Uncle Emmet made us take the county road.

We liked the hill route best because when we took it it meant that we could look at our traps on the way to and from school. By mid-December we'd trapped seven weasel, two mink, and a muskrat. The weasel and mink were already dead when we took them out of the traps, but the muskrat wasn't. It had dragged its trap into the bushes and was snarling and clawing. I had to kill it because I was the older.

It was the hardest thing I ever had to do, and I would have been willing to give up trapping for good that morning if I hadn't been afraid Uncle Emmet and Mort would think I was a coward. Besides, Mort had spent one whole Sunday helping us look for animal tracks on creek banks and under overhanging willow branches and showing us how to bait and set the traps. He'd taught us how to skin out our catches and put the pelts on stretchers, too. He'd even turned over some of his own traps to us. I couldn't bear to disappoint Mort, so I got a big rock and killed the muskrat. After that first time it was never so hard to kill a trapped animal again, but it never was easy either.

As the cold increased we were glad we had our fur-lined mittens and overshoes and fleece-lined coats. Even so, our feet and hands would sometimes be numb before we reached school, and once my cheeks got frostbitten. I don't think we realized how cruel cold could be though, until one morning we found a beautiful Chinese pheasant lying dead and frozen to the ground in a quaking-aspen grove near the school.

Uncle Emmet said pheasant roosted on the ground, and the warmth of their bodies often melted the snow, so that when it froze again they were trapped. After that morning we always looked for pheasant on our way to school, and if we found any trapped in ice we'd break it and turn them loose. Bastian gave us chunks of suet to feed them, and the pheasant got to know us and look for us. They'd come strutting along in the snow when they heard our horses. They finally got so tame they'd take the suet from our fingers.

School let out for the holidays on December twenty-first, and that same day Mother's Christmas box came in the mail. We'd been waiting for Uncle Emmet to say something about a Christmas tree, but I don't believe he ever would have thought of it if Mother hadn't sent a lot of ornaments, some tinsel, and a Christmas angel in her box.

"Women's trappings!" Uncle Emmet snorted when he saw us unpacking the angel. But he must have seen how unhappy we looked, because later that day he told us to take Dolly and the sled and go up on the mountain and chop down a tree.

"You're too old for such foolishness," he said, "but we can't disappoint your ma. She's going to feel bad enough being away from you at Christmas."

That same afternoon we got a beautiful tree that reached clear to the ceiling, and it was a good thing we did, because we couldn't possibly have got up the mountain again for a week to come.

That night a blizzard began, and when we woke up the next morning the wind was howling and the snow had piled halfway up the downstairs windows. All over the house the windows were frosted, so that we couldn't see out unless we scratched a peephole in solid ice. Every stove in the house was going full blast, and the big dining-room stove had rosy spots on its pot-bellied sides. We stayed close to it most of the morning, cleaning our guns, mending traps, and playing canasta.

The next day the storm got worse and the thermometer dropped to forty below zero. Icicles several feet long hung from the eaves of the house. When the men came in for breakfast, ice formed by their breath clung to their whiskers and eyebrows, and their faces were red with cold.

Uncle Emmet was worried about the sheep. "Can't hope for a letup," he said, turning away from the barometer. He told us he seldom fed the sheep so early in the winter, and never did as long as they could paw through the snow to grass. "If the snow crusts up we got to haul feed to the camps."

By the next morning a heavy crust had formed over the snow, and right after breakfast all hands, except Bastian, loaded cottonseed cake and hay and bedrolls on trucks and wagons and set out for the camps.

As Uncle Emmet hoisted his bedroll to his shoulder, Dan looked like he was going to cry. "Tomorrow's Christmas Eve," he said real low.

"So it is," Uncle Emmet said loudly, turning up his coat collar.

"Will you be back in time to help us trim our tree?" I wanted to know. All of a sudden I thought I couldn't bear to have him go. We'd never been away from home at Christmas. Suppose he didn't get back in time! I swallowed a lump in my throat.

"I'll get back as quick as I can," he promised. "And don't you kids leave this house till the storm lets up."

All morning the wind howled and hurled huge chunks of snow through the air. By noon the fence was completely hidden by drifts, and an hour later when we looked through the peepholes we'd made earlier in the windows we couldn't see anything but a solid curtain of whirling snow.

"Are you sure the men can find their way back?" I asked Bastian.

"Oh sure," he said, "they'll follow the fences home if it gets too bad."

At five o'clock Bastian got a pail and said he'd have to go to the barn to feed the horses and milk. He was gone so long that we were afraid he'd had an accident and needed help. We were just getting into our coats and mittens when he burst breathlessly through the kitchen door.

"You crazy kids!" he shouted, putting the milk pail on the table. "I'll wring your necks if I catch you getting ready to go out in this storm again—for any reason! You understand?"

"We thought you might have got hurt," I explained meekly, "and might freeze to death out there."

"So you thought you'd come freeze with me?" But he was pleased just the same to think we liked him that well, and he told us stories until bedtime. And when we started upstairs he called after us, "Tomorrow we'll make some colored popcorn balls to go on your Christmas tree. And we might string some cranberries too."

I knew he was just trying to make us feel better about Christmas in case Uncle Emmet didn't get home. But next morning, the morning of Christmas Eve, he got really interested and even made a gingerbread tree to put on the dining-room table, and a big batch of colored cookies.

At four o'clock Bastian said, "Look, kids, if the boss was going to get back, he'd be here by now. He ain't coming, so let's get busy and trim that tree."

We'd been hopeful about Uncle Emmet's return until then, and now we both felt so sad we weren't much interested in the tree any more. But after Bastian made a standard and set it up and put the angel on the top of the tree we felt a little better. He helped us for a while; then he put on his coat and overshoes and told us he was going to turn the calves in with the cows. "We got too much milk anyway—with the crew all gone."

If we'd lived long on a ranch we'd have known better than that. But we never suspected that the reason Bastian was going to turn the calves in with the cows was because he knew he could never get back to the house with a full pail of milk.

"I'll be back in fifteen minutes," he told us; and warned, "Don't you kids stick your noses out of that door while I'm gone. Hear me?"

We promised, not knowing how soon the promise would have to be broken.

We finished trimming the tree, and put the presents under it. Mother had sent something for everybody—there was even a box for Molly. We'd ordered our presents from Sears Roebuck, and we got so interested in wrapping them and writing the cards that we didn't notice the time until the clock struck six. Bastian had been gone more than an hour. At six-thirty we really began to worry, and Molly made it worse because she started to whine and run up and down in front of the door. Had something happened to Bastian? Had Molly sensed it?

Dan and I looked at each other. We both must have had the same thought because he said, "We promised Bastian we wouldn't go out."

"We've *got* to break the promise," I said, already getting into my coat.

A few minutes later we opened the door. It took both of us to close it, and we knew right away that we could never find the barn. We couldn't see a foot ahead of us, and besides, the wind was so strong we could hardly stand up. We had to hang on to each other. We went back inside and talked it over.

"We've got to go," I told Dan.

"It's like Bastian said, though," Dan replied. "We'd never get to the barn, and then all three of us would freeze. I wonder—" Suddenly he snapped his fingers. "Jack, remember that story we read about the woman who got to her barn in a blizzard by tying a rope to the door and taking it along with her? Remember, she had to start out several times and come back before she found the barn, but she finally made it?"

It seemed like a wonderful idea, but then I remembered that all the rope was in the barn, and said so.

"But there's a big ball of strong twine in the basement," Dan said. "I saw it when Bastian was tying up bunches of onions."

We raced down the cellar stairs, found the cord, and tied one end of it to the door. Then we jumped off the porch into the snow. It reached almost to our knees, and the wind took our breath for a minute, so we had to hold tightly to each other before we could start. We finally ducked our heads and plunged on.

When we got to the fence we climbed right over it on the drifts. The snow must have been six feet deep, and we were out of breath again before we made the other side and looked back. It gave me a queer, scared feeling not to be able to see the lights we'd left in the kitchen. Not to see anything—

I took Dan's hand. He was shivering with cold. We couldn't talk to each other because the wind tore the words right out of our mouths and blew them away. I was doling out the cord, and after a while I couldn't feel the ball in my hands. For an awful second I thought I'd lost it, but when I raised my hand to my face it was still there. It was a relief to know that my hands were just numb with cold.

I was walking ahead, with Dan hanging on to my coat, and suddenly I bumped into something. It was an old sheep wagon, down the creek and out of line with the barn. We stood in its shelter a little while, trying to decide whether it would be better to go back to the house and start out again or edge our way along the bank of the creek until we found the bridge. We decided to try for the bridge. If we found that we were sure we could make the barn.

I don't know how we ever found the bridge in that howling wind and drifting snow, but after what seemed hours we finally did. We had to get down on our hands and knees and crawl over the cattle guard that led into the barnyard. From here it was easier, because the guard was in a straight line with the gate that led into the corral. We climbed the drifts that covered the fence, calling Bastian all the while. This was silly because he couldn't have heard us. We couldn't hear each other.

We found Bastian the minute we shoved the big door open. He was huddled on the floor near a manger. There was blood all over his face and head, and his leg was doubled up under him. His eyes were closed and his breath came in gasps. His face—the parts where there wasn't any blood—looked blue in the dim light of a lantern that hung from one of the stalls. We knelt down and shook him, calling his name over and over. He just lay there, breathing that funny way.

"He'll freeze to death if he stays here much longer!" Dan was crying, but then, I was crying too. It all seemed so hopeless. It was easy to see that Bastian's leg was broken.

We couldn't leave him. We couldn't drag him back to the house. It had been all we could do to get ourselves over the drifts on the fences. I stood up and leaned against one of the stalls, feeling dizzy and sick.

Suddenly something moist and warm touched my cheek. It was Dolly, and she was nuzzling me and making funny little snuffles. It was as if she were trying to comfort me and tell me something. She did tell me something, because I remembered what Uncle Emmet had said about pack horses being willing to go anywhere they were led.

I threw my arms around Dolly's neck and hugged her. "We can hitch Dolly to the sled and haul Bastian back to the house," I told Dan excitedly.

After we'd hitched Dolly each of us took one of Bastian's arms and dragged him onto the sled. I led Dolly, and rerolled the cord on the ball as we went forward. Dan braced Bastian's body on the sled.

To this day I don't know how we got back to the house, and we never would have if Dolly hadn't been such a grand old mare, so willing to do her part. Twice when we went over drifted fences Dan was thrown off, and each time Dolly stood still until he scrambled back onto the sled.

In the end it was Dolly who guided us back to the house—after I'd lost the ball of twine. It slipped from my numb fingers as I was trying to wind it. Terrified, I dug around in the snow, and when I couldn't find the twine I became panic-stricken. Dragging on Dolly's halter, I began to run. We would have missed the house and probably frozen but for the good old mare. She balked near the gate and refused to go on. I jerked at the halter, lost my footing, and stumbled against a post. Then I was conscious of a faint haze of light through the snow. We were home! Dolly had known the way all along! I was glad to remember that she'd have no trouble getting back to the barn when, a few moments later, we unbuckled her harness.

I'll never forget how wonderful the warmth and light of the kitchen seemed when we went inside.

We dragged a mattress down in front of the stove, near the Christmas tree, put Bastian on it, and covered him with blankets. Then Dan got a cup of coffee from the pot that was always on the back of the stove, and we forced it through Bastian's blue lips spoonful by spoonful.

We were washing the blood from his face when he opened his eyes and tried to sit up. "I thought I'd died and gone to heaven," he told us later. "The first thing I saw was that angel on top of the tree!"

We made him lie back and wouldn't let him talk for a while. When he'd had another cup of coffee he told us he'd gone to the loft to pitch down some hay and must have slipped through the opening and hit his head on a post as he fell. (Uncle Emmet told us later that Bastian's bad eye made him clumsy, and that was why he was a cook instead of a ranch hand.)

"If you hadn't come I'd of been a gone gosling for sure," Bastian said sheepishly. Then, in the next breath, "You crazy kids! I told you not to leave this house! Why'd you do it? You might've froze to death!"

We couldn't help giggling then, and after a minute

Bastian grinned too. We could tell his leg hurt him terribly, though he made light of it, said it wasn't anything, that he'd broken legs before and Uncle Emmet could set it as soon as he got in. He said Uncle Emmet was as good as a doctor when it came to setting bones.

Bastian told us what to fix for supper. There was a big pot of mulligan stew and some beans already cooked and we warmed them up. We were washing the dishes when we heard a commotion outside, and Molly began to run back and forth, barking furiously. Uncle Emmet and the men had come home! We knew it before they burst through the door.

"We broke two springs on one truck, and the other's snowed in ten miles upcountry," Mort told us. "Never seen the boss so set on gettin' home. If the buckboard had got busted he'd likely have made us hoof it back."

That made me feel all warm and happy because I knew why Uncle Emmet had been determined to get home. We heated the mulligan stew and beans again and the men ate supper. Then Mort and Uncle Emmet set Bastian's leg. We stayed in the kitchen, clearing up while they did it, and Bastian didn't make a sound. But after it was over he told Uncle Emmet what had happened, and how we'd disobeyed him and come out to the barn. "Crazy kids!" he kept saying. "They might of froze."

We were afraid Uncle Emmet was going to scold

us for not doing as we were told. But he didn't. He
came to the kitchen door and just stood there looking
at us for a minute as if he wanted to say something. But
just then the clock struck twelve, and what he said
was, "Merry Christmas!"

It was a wonderful Christmas after all. Uncle
Emmet told everyone to open his presents and sleep
late the next day. Mother sent all the men hand-
knitted mufflers, and there was a new collar for Molly.
Dan and I got fishing rods from Mother and Dad, and
everything to go with them—nets, hooks, flies, and a
waterproof box for the tackle. The men and Uncle
Emmet were very pleased with our gifts of wool
socks, and the four men had chipped in together and
bought Dan and me each a beautiful silver concho
belt. But Uncle Emmet hadn't given us anything. He's
already given us so much, I kept telling myself. And
he'd broken two trucks and ridden back in an open
buckboard just to make it in time for our Christmas—

And then it happened. When all the gifts had been
opened and the men were getting ready to leave,
Uncle Emmet went into his office and came out with
two saddles, hand-carved and trimmed with real silver
conchos! We knew he must have bought them weeks
before and smuggled them into his office. And he'd
said Christmas was foolishness!

19. Wool-blind Sheep

After Christmas things seemed to change at the ranch, as far as Dan and I were concerned, anyway. The men had always been good to us, but they'd treated us like a couple of kids. After Christmas they talked to us as they talked to one another, and they'd call on us to do chores that only the men had done before.

"We must be learning to be ranchers," I told Uncle Emmet one Saturday morning, "because Bill took us along to move some sheep last Saturday and today Shorty wants us to help him collect some canvas dams he left in the field, then help mend a fence."

Uncle Emmet didn't speak for a minute; then he said quietly, "You boys earned your spurs. You earned them Christmas Eve when you hauled Bastian in from the barn. Mighty few kids would have had your foresight. There ain't a man on this place wouldn't trust you to do the right thing now."

I was very proud for a minute, and then I knew it would be cheating if I didn't tell Uncle Emmet how scared we'd been.

He said, "Rats! Who wouldn't be scared? I'd have been scared myself!" After that I felt as though I'd grown a foot taller.

We could hardly wait for the week-ends during January. Every Saturday we helped some of the men with some job that we knew was men's work.

It was still bitterly cold, and there was a lot of snow, but the roads and the trails had packed down until the trucks were able to get over them. We helped Mort tend camp. He'd give us the herders' lists and we'd fill them from supplies in the basement and load them into the buckboard. Sometimes, when there weren't too many things to take and the camp was near, Mort would let us pack the supplies in saddlebags and take them up on our horses.

Bill let us help him too. He took care of the hospital band—weak or old sheep that couldn't forage for themselves and had been brought to the home ranch to be fed. Before January was over Bill said we could handle the afternoon feeding alone. He'd have the wagon loaded with hay when we got home from school and we'd take turns driving the team and pitching off the feed.

One Saturday in early February Uncle Emmet said he was going to bring some sheep to the home ranch that day and we could help.

"More hospital sheep?" I asked.

"No," he said, "I'm going to cut out the wool-blind ewes and bring them back here to be eyed."

We'd never heard of this operation before and wanted to know all about it. On the way to the first camp Uncle Emmet told us that cold weather made wool grow fast, and during the winter it grew thickest around the ewes' eyes. Then the snow and ice would force it down like a curtain, and unless it was sheared away the sheep would become wool-blind and unable to graze or follow the herd.

He told us that snow was hard on the herders' eyes too, and that the glare sometimes caused them to lose their sight temporarily.

"Most herders wear dark-lensed glasses," Uncle Emmet said.

Then he told us a story about one of his herders who lost his glasses and became snow-blind. "He was herding close to camp, or he'd never have made it back to the wagon. He was laid up three days, and his sheep scattered and mixed with a half-dozen other ranchers' herds. Took us weeks to round them up. Nicky belonged to that flock and was missing for months. I never expected to see the rascal again."

Uncle Emmet said that sheepherders know the brands of the different sheepmen, and when strays wander into their herds they're supposed to report it to their bosses so the rightful owner can be notified.

But Nicky was the prize bell sheep of the whole country, and when he wandered into a herd the sheepherder recognized him at once. He'd seen him work at the stockyards, and he wanted him. He kept Nicky so long that his brand wore off and there was no way to tell him from the rest of the sheep.

Months later Uncle Emmet was riding past one of his neighbor's herds and thought he recognized Nicky. He stopped and spoke to the herder. "That looks like my bellwether," he said.

The herder said right away that it wasn't Nicky; it was a wether he'd raised from a lamb. He said it so convincingly that Uncle Emmet couldn't be certain. But he knew that if this was Nicky there must be more of his sheep in the herd. He hated to put the owner of the flock to the trouble of corralling the sheep and running them through a dodge gate unless he had something more to go on.

He remembered Nicky's weakness for tobacco, so he got out a package of cigarettes, held it above his head, and shouted, "Hi! Nicky!" Nicky practically stampeded the herd in getting to Uncle Emmet, and there was nothing the herder could do then but admit that Nicky had strayed into his herd months before and brought sixteen ewes with him.

When Uncle Emmet went to the owner about the mixup the man laughed and said, "Well, that explains everything. Ike's so stingy he'll hardly buy himself clothes. He switched from sack tobacco to tailor-mades, and till now I never could figure out why."

Uncle Emmet told us interesting stories about strayed sheep the whole ten miles to the first camp, and somehow when he was talking he made us feel as if we were a part of the ranch. He'd say, "our sheep," "our dogs," "our herders," and when we got in sight of the camp he said, "Well, fellers, there's our first camp."

It was easy to cut out the wool-blind sheep. They had little curtains of wool down over their eyes and were clumsy and couldn't move fast. There were five hundred of them, and when they were cut out and counted Uncle Emmet surprised us by saying, "You kids take over here and move this bunch to the ranch. I'm not cutting any more sheep today, but I want to look over the range upcountry."

I guess we'll remember that as the proudest moment of our lives. Uncle Emmet had given us a real job, a man's job. He'd trusted us with five hundred of his best ewes, worth thousands of dollars. I don't think we could have stood it if we'd lost even one sheep on the way home. I know we counted the five black markers at least a hundred times, and we got to the ranch house at sundown with exactly the number of sheep we'd started out with.

20. Beaver Dams

We trapped until April. Then, just before lambing, Mort told us the pelts were no longer prime and we might just as well pull our traps for the season. We'd been lucky, and when the fur buyer came by we sold our furs for a hundred and twenty-five dollars. We'd never seen this much money in cash before, much less earned it, and for days we couldn't think or talk of anything except how we'd spend the money.

We finally agreed we'd buy something for Dad's birthday, which was April twentieth. After that we spent most of the time we weren't in school poring over mail-order catalogues. Uncle Emmet and every one of the men were just as interested as we in our selection. They made all kinds of suggestions, and the choice finally narrowed down to a gun or a wrist watch.

We wrote Mother, and she thought Dad would like the gun better. She said he'd been trying to write an article for a sports magazine and had got very discouraged. "Maybe the gun will cheer him up and get him interested again," she wrote, "and it might help if you boys wrote him about hunting trips you'd like to take with him when he gets well." Imagine Mother's writing this!

So we ordered the gun. When it came and we unwrapped it we knew Dad couldn't help but be thrilled. It was a .303-caliber Savage with a telescope sight, and every man on the place said it was a dandy.

We sent it to San Francisco the very next day and could hardly wait to hear from Mother. But the letter, when it came, was from Dad—the first letter we'd had from him since we'd heard that he was missing somewhere in Korea! He wrote:

Fellows, you'll never know what that gun means to me. I just sit and look at it, and whenever a doctor or nurse stops to admire it I say casually (but you'll never know how proud I feel inside), "Birthday gift from my two sons. They bought it with money they earned trapping out on a ranch in Montana."

He said we'd plan a hunting trip in the Ozarks as soon as he got on his feet.

"I wish it could be in Montana," Dan said to Uncle Emmet, "so you could go too."

"Who knows?" he replied. "Might happen some-day. A writing fellow like your dad ought to be able to write one place as well as another."

We missed trapping. We'd been so interested in it that it was hard to put it out of our minds all of a sud-den. So we started visiting a ridge above the canyon around dusk to watch the beavers play on their slide. They were getting too thick again, Mort told us. And it was almost time to turn the irrigation water into the ditches.

"When that happens I got to tear out this dam. Want to help me?" he asked. Then he pointed down. "See that big old beaver swimmin' 'round so impor-tant-like just under the edge of the willows? That's Sassy."

He scratched his head. "I got to figure out some way to get the best of her. Once lambing starts I won't have time to tear out a dam every few days."

As soon as Shorty had cleared the irrigation ditches of rocks and branches and leaves we helped Mort rip out the beaver dam. That night Shorty had a fine head of water rushing along the creek to the ditches.

More regarded it gloomily. "There won't be a trickle in a few days. Old Sassy and her crew'll be on the job again and have that dam back in place before you can say Jack Robinson."

We couldn't believe it, but when we went up the canyon three days later the dam was back, and only a thin trickle of water ran down the creek. We tore Sassy's dam out twice, and then one morning Mort called us aside and confided, "I've thought of a way to outsmart the old sister. I ain't goin' to tear out any more of her dams, and ain't she goin' to be surprised!"

He showed us a length of six-inch pipe and explained that he meant to dive into the pond backed up by the dam and drive the pipe through from one side to the other.

"I'm goin' to fasten it in place with some two-foot iron spikes. Then let's see her move them. Tomorrow morning," he boasted, "you're goin' to see a full head of water movin' through that pipe down the creek, and Sassy won't have enough water to flip her tail in."

We could hardly wait until morning to see if he was right, and soon after breakfast the three of us hurried up the canyon. Mort was chuckling all the way, but when we came in sight of the dam I never saw a funnier look on anybody's face. It was the creek that had only a trickle of water, and the pond beyond was full to the brim!

Mort said some words that Mother wouldn't have been pleased to hear. He shucked out of his clothes and dived down into that icy water. When he finally came up he was blue with cold and mad as a hornet.

"Know what she's done?" he sputtered, shivering as he got hurriedly into his clothes. "She's plugged that pipe with willow branches and leaves and mud tight as she can cram it all the way through to the other side —a whole four feet! I'll bet she's giving me the hee-haw from somewhere up in those bushes."

He gave his sock a vicious jerk. "I give up. I'll have to tell the boss and let him take over."

We'd thought Uncle Emmet would be mad when Mort told him how he'd protected Sassy. But Uncle Emmet just threw back his head and shouted with laughter. And the funny thing was, he protected Sassy too, because when the game warden brought in some trappers Uncle Emmet looked over their catch every time, and when they got Sassy he made them turn her and her youngest kittens loose.

"I think Mort kind of likes her," he told us. "And I don't mind having a few beaver around, myself."

21. Coyotes at Lambing Time

Lambing began the first week in May. For three weeks before this the Rising Arrow was the busiest place I'd ever seen. The ewes were brought in to the home ranch to be tagged—that is, to have the ragged tags of wool sheared away from their bags so the lambs wouldn't choke on them or get sick. Then the hauling began. Day after day trucks loaded with cottonseed cake, salt, hay, and food supplies went back and forth from the ranch. The tents were checked over and mended by two men who came out from town and brought their sewing machines with them.

One afternoon when we got home from school we found Mort loading the tents on a truck. "Give me a hand here," he said, "and I'll let you ride up to the lambing camp with me."

He loaded the big tents, and we loaded some tepees so small that we wondered how a man could double up enough to get inside, much less sleep in one. But they weren't for the men.

"If a ewe won't suckle her lamb," Mort said, "we

shut her up in the tepee with it until she decides to be a good mother. There's nothing like a fill of warm milk to put a newborn lamb on its feet." He grinned. "But sometimes a ewe gets ornery and walks off like the lamb's no business of hers. A few hours in a tepee'll cure her."

The tepees were also used for flagging, he told us.

"Flagging?" I pictured a man waving the tepee like a flag.

"How could they use that heavy piece of canvas for a flag?" Dan asked.

Mort really laughed then, and said that flagging meant putting a lighted lantern in a tepee to scare the coyotes away. "The pesky things always stalk a drop-band (ewes to be lambed) in the hopes of getting a lamb, but they won't come near a light."

"Can't a ewe protect her lamb?"

"How can she, without any horns or teeth?"

"No teeth?"

"None that'll do her any good for fighting off coyotes. The only teeth a ewe's got in her upper jaw are the grinders way back in her mouth."

Mort said if a ewe did put up a fight it was just too bad, because then the coyote killed both the ewe and the lamb.

"If you boys stick around this summer maybe the boss'll let you poison coyotes. They're thicker'n flies this year."

We couldn't stick around. Mother had already written that the doctors said Dad could go back to Springfield in June, and she planned to have us meet them in Salt Lake City. We wanted to see Mother and Dad real bad, but we couldn't bear to think about leaving the Rising Arrow. We didn't like to talk about it, so both Dan and I got quiet after that. Mort went on talking about coyotes, the damage they did to sheep, and how they could be killed or trapped.

He said the best way to get rid of them was by using poisoned bait.

"Oats?" I asked, remembering the gopher bait.

"Heck no! Most trappers use the carcass of a cow or horse that's been treated with a mixture of arsenic and strychnine. They haul it up to a place where the coyotes are thick, and it'll get 'em every time. But they got to be careful to put it where sheep dogs won't get at it too—they go after the bait just the same as the coyotes."

Then he told us about the way trappers forced coyote pups out of their dens. They'd find a den and drag the pups out with a length of barbed wire doubled and twisted so that one end formed a loop that wouldn't slip from the hand. The opposite end was bent into two prongs.

"Then the trapper just pushes the prongs into the den and fishes around with them until they tangle in a pup's fur. They can drag them out as easy as pie after that. Too bad you ain't goin' to be here this summer," he said. "You could sure make you a real stake—good as you've got to be at trappin'. The government pays a bounty for the coyote, and the sheepmen match it."

"Well, we're not going to be here," I said unhappily.

It was suppertime when we got back to the ranch. Old Molly ran out and greeted us, whining and licking our hands. We loved Molly now, and Thunder and Lightning had become just like a couple of friends. It wouldn't be long before we'd have to leave them. I couldn't even bear to think about it. I wished we didn't have to go to school so we could spend every minute we had left on the ranch.

22. Jacketing a Lamb

We hadn't expected to see much of the lambing.

Dan complained, "Everybody else'll go to the lambing camp and we'll be stuck in the schoolroom." But we got a break. Mrs. Morton had to go to teachers' meeting in Bozeman early in May, and we had a holiday from Wednesday until Monday.

Uncle Emmet was almost as pleased as we were. "I could use a couple of extra hands," he said.

Tuesday night we tied up our bedrolls and set out to the first lambing camp with Uncle Emmet. There were two camps, with eight lambers each. We questioned Uncle Emmet most of the way, eager to know what our jobs would be. He told us we'd tepee ewes and lambs part of the day and flag the rest. We were glad Mort had explained all of this to us when Uncle Emmet said, his eyes twinkling, "Bet you don't know any more now than before you asked."

"Bet we do!" Dan laughed and told him. We all three laughed then, but after a minute Uncle Emmet's face grew serious, and he said, "You kids are on the right track. I always figure the best way to learn a business is to listen and look."

We didn't have much time to listen the rest of the week. We had to be ready at any minute to set up a tepee and wrangle a ewe and a lamb inside. And after the second day the lambers turned even the most ornery ewes over to us, and we'd throw them and force them to let their lambs suck. We had to take care of the lanterns for flagging too—polish their chimneys and fill them with oil so they'd be ready for use in the late afternoon.

At night we were so tired we could scarcely move, but we never could fall into bed until we'd picked the sheep ticks off each other. The wood ticks were thick too, and we were glad Mother didn't know about this, because she'd have worried for fear we'd get spotted fever.

After the second day Uncle Emmet brought our rifles up from the ranch and told us to shoot every magpie we saw. The magpies were pretty and friendly, and we hated to do this until we saw one dart down and pick out the eyes of a newborn lamb. Uncle Emmet said magpies blinded any number of lambs every year. After that we shot every one we could and never minded a bit.

We were kept so busy we didn't have time to watch a lamber "jacket" a lamb until Sunday. We knew about jacketing because Uncle Emmet had a picture of a jacketed lamb on the wall of his office. It was the queerest-looking creature, with four normal legs and another four that dangled above them.

Uncle Emmet had teased us when we asked him about it. "Mean to say you never saw an eight-legged lamb?"

But after a while he'd told us that if you made a profit at lambing you had to be sure that every ewe with a bagful of milk had a lamb to suckle. When a ewe lost her lamb, he said, she had to be persuaded to suckle a twin, or orphan, and she wasn't easy persuaded. Sometimes she'd trample the strange lamb and kill it. She knew the scent of her lamb and refused to adopt another. So the sheepmen figured out a way to trick her. They skinned her dead lamb and put its pelt on the orphan or twin.

Sunday morning we were tepeeing a ewe and her lamb near a lamber who was getting ready to jacket. He slit the pelt of the dead lamb along the hind side and peeled it off as quick and easy as you'd take off a sweater. Then he shook the jacket right side out, made slits in the legs and a slit at the neck.

When the jacket was ready he picked up a twin lamb, poked its knobby legs through the slits and its head through the hole at the neck. I've never seen a funnier sight. Two tails, eight legs, and a ragged pelt that looked as though it was peeling. Dan and I shouted with laughter.

We didn't think the ewe was smart, though. She stood right there and watched the whole thing, bleating and pawing the earth all the while. But she let the lamber foist the twin lamb off on her. She looked startled, and tried to escape when he grabbed her leg and forced her to let the funny little creature suckle. After a minute she caught the scent of her own lamb from the jacket, sniffed several times, then stopped struggling. She actually believed the adopted lamb was her own!

We had to go back to school on Monday, and that week seemed to stretch out endlessly, but Friday afternoon finally came and we again loaded our bedrolls on the truck and went back to our jobs at the lambing camp.

We learned more about sheep that month than we'd learned the whole year we'd been at the Rising Arrow. We learned that they are curious and want to see everything that is going on. For instance, when a ewe couldn't give birth to her lamb alone and the lamber had to help her, the other ewes would stand in a semicircle, watching the operation like a bunch of curious old women. They'd do the same thing when a ewe and her lamb had to be tepeed or when a lamb got fitted with a jacket.

We learned too that ewes are devoted mothers once they've accepted their lambs. Time and again we saw ewes standing above their dead lambs, bleating pitifully. At first they all looked alike to us, but after we'd worked with them for a while their faces all looked different—just like people's.

When we mentioned this to Uncle Emmet he was more pleased than I'd ever seen him before. " 'Tain't everybody can see that in sheep," he said and clapped us on our backs, "only born sheepmen. I wish I could keep you kids up here for another year. I'd have me a couple of partners!"

The lambs were docked—had their tails cut off— one Saturday, and we knew that Uncle Emmet had set that date just so we could be on hand. We helped wrangle the ewes and lambs into a corral; then Uncle Emmet stood at a dodge gate and cut the ewes into one corral and the lambs into another.

We caught the lambs and handed them to the docker. It made me rather sick to see him whack their tails off with a red-hot chisel and turn them over to another man who doctored the stumps with sheep dip. But I don't think it hurt the lambs but a minute. They didn't act as if it did, anyway.

After all the lambs were docked they were turned back in the corral to mother-up with the ewes. There was an awful commotion and noise for a few minutes —until the lambs found their mothers and began to suckle. Then there wasn't a sound.

23. Two Surprises

School would be out the last day of May. As the time drew near we wondered why we'd ever wished it would be out so soon. When school closed we'd have to say good-by to Uncle Emmet, and all the men, and our ponies, and Molly.

"You ain't sickenin', are you?" Bastian asked at breakfast the last day of school. I hadn't eaten but one flapjack, and usually I ate four, and some eggs and bacon and cereal besides. Dan hadn't eaten much either. I couldn't answer Bastian and I couldn't swallow. I felt as if I were going to cry, so I got up quickly and ran out to the barn. While I was saddling Lightning, Dan and Uncle Emmet came into the corral.

Uncle Emmet did a few chores; then he walked over to us and said, "I'm going to Dillon on business tomorrow. How'd you fellows like to ride along?"

I didn't want to go, and I could see that Dan didn't either. We'd be taking a train from there in a few days anyway, and I didn't even want to think about it.

"I'd rather not, sir," I said. "We'll have to pack our

suitcases, and besides, I want to ride Lightning every minute I can until we have to leave."

"The packing can wait. You'd better come along with me to Dillon. It's a long, lonesome ride for a fellow to take alone."

After that we couldn't refuse, but I felt a little cross with Uncle Emmet for dragging us away from the Rising Arrow when we had so little time left.

Besides, the men were getting ready for shearing, and Mort had promised we could ride up to the shearing pens with him the next afternoon. We hated to miss the shearing, and wished Mother had let us stay just another two weeks. Now that we knew the ropes we felt it would have been even more fun than last year.

Both Dan and I had made good grades in school, Mrs. Morton said, and she added, "I wish I could have you boys next year."

That last day of school we rode home real slow and stopped to look at all the places we'd set traps during the winter. As we got near the house Dan asked the question that had been churning around in my mind for a month. "Do you suppose we'll ever get to come back?"

I doubted it, and shook my head. Montana and Missouri were hundreds of miles apart. It cost money for four people to travel, and we'd never had too much of that.

The next morning we went to Dillon. The day had even begun wrong. We'd thought Uncle Emmet wouldn't leave until afternoon, giving us a chance to ride Thunder and Lightning before we started out. But Uncle Emmet hustled us off right after breakfast. "I've got some important business in Dillon," he said.

We didn't think it could be too important, because when we got there he talked fifteen minutes to a sheepherder he met on the street. Then he headed straight for the Andrus Hotel and said, "I'm going to get a room so you kids'll have a place to loaf while I'm nosing around."

I said we'd rather just sit in the lobby and wait, but he shook his head. For the first time since I'd known him I was really mad at Uncle Emmet. He'd known all the while that there wasn't anything to do in Dillon —not even a movie to go to until night.

So Dan and I were both feeling sulky when we followed him into the elevator and down the hall on the second floor. When he got to a corner room he opened a door. At first we thought we'd walked into somebody else's room. There was a man lying on one of the beds.

The man shouted, "Hi, fellows!" and held out his arms. We were so surprised we couldn't speak or move. We just stood there gaping. The man was our dad! Then Mother came flying out of the bathroom, and the four of us were hugging one another and laughing like idiots. Uncle Emmet still stood in the door with his Stetson in his hand, and after a minute Mother saw him and dashed over and hugged him and kissed him too.

Then Mother put her arms around Dan and me and said in a shaky little voice, "Boys, we've come to spend the whole summer. And you owe this grand surprise to your uncle. He telephoned me a week ago and insisted that we come. He even sent us the money for our train fares."

"Not on your life I didn't!" Uncle Emmet boomed. "The boys sent you that two hundred dollars! They earned every cent of it lambing, and I still owe them a hundred more."

I don't think we were ever so happy. We knew the wages the men were getting, and Uncle Emmet was paying us men's wages for the days we'd worked. And besides, he somehow made us feel that we'd earned it. This time, whether he liked it or not, we both flung ourselves at him and hugged him.

He got sort of red in the face and backed away, but we hung right on. He threw up his arms, looked at Mother, and grinned. "Well, you two dudes may have plenty of time to palaver, but these ranch hands and me got to get back to the Rising Arrow. We got no time to waste. We got plenty of chores to do there."